MICHAEL HARDCASTLE

SOCCER SPECIAL

Mammoth

First published in Great Britain 1978
by Methuen Children's Books Ltd
Published 1978 by Magnet
Published 1990 by Mammoth
Reissued 1998 by Mammoth
an imprint of Reed International Books Limited
Michelin House, 81 Fulham Road, London SW3 6RB

Text copyright © 1978 Michael Hardcastle
Illustrations copyright © 1978 Paul Wright

The moral rights of the author and illustrator have been asserted.

ISBN 0 7497 0705 4

10 9 8 7 6 5 4 3 2 1

A CIP catalogue record for this title
is available from the British Library

Printed and bound in Great Britain
by Cox & Wyman Ltd, Reading, Berkshire

One

Miles Hansen remembered how the ball had bounced right in front of the centre-forward. It was just outside the penalty area. Geoff Leyland had trapped it, dummied past an opponent and then pushed the ball to his inside-right. When the return pass came Geoff hit the ball first time – and it went into the net off the upright. It really was a very good goal.

Miles nodded to himself. That was exactly how it had been scored. He had a good memory and he also had the notes he'd scribbled down at the match itself. Now he was going to write about the game and describe Geoff Leyland's goal.

The story would appear in his own newspaper, *Soccer Special*, along with reports of other matches and items of football news that he'd collected during the week. It would be printed the following day and Miles would sell all the copies himself at 2p a copy. Geoff would probably buy two copies – maybe even three –

because his name appeared several times. Geoff liked to read about himself.

Every word in the newspaper was written by Miles himself, without help from anyone, and so it took quite a long time to produce. But he enjoyed the work. He could write about whatever he liked. There was nobody to tell him what to do or how to do it. If he thought that someone had played badly he could say so; if a centre-forward missed an absolute sitter he could put it in the paper like that: 'the centre-forward missed an absolute sitter'.

Miles believed that a newspaper reporter should be completely honest and accurate in everything he wrote. His readers wanted facts, not fantasy. Miles always gave them the facts in *Soccer Special*. That was one of the reasons why his newspaper was so popular. Readers knew that they were getting the truth.

The paper wasn't only about football, however; it also contained news about his friends and family and neighbours. It was those items which helped to sell the paper. Geoff Leyland wasn't the only one who liked to read about himself. Miles' parents and his sister and the people who lived in the same street all wanted to see what he'd written about them. Every time a new edition of the paper came out they were all willing to pay 2p for a copy.

Miles called his newspaper *Soccer Special* because he liked the title – and because he liked football more than anything else in the world. He wished he could play in a football team and score lots of goals. He'd rather play centre-forward for England than become Editor of the *Daily Express*. But there was no chance of that happening. For Miles didn't play football.

When he was younger he'd had many ill-nesses, some of them very severe ones, including rheumatic fever. Twice he'd been in hospital and on the second occasion, when he'd had his tonsils removed, he was kept in even over the Christmas holiday. While he was recovering from his last illness he'd actually made a list of all the diseases and infections he'd suffered from in recent years. His sister, peering over his shoulder as he completed it, remarked in a hor-rified tone, 'Goodness, what a list! It frightens me to death just to read it.'

During his attack of rheumatic fever the family's doctor had said that it might be best if Miles didn't play any really energetic sports until he was older. Miles' mother had never forgotten that. Even though the doctor had sent an official note to the school she sometimes sent notes to the sports master to remind him that Miles was not well enough to play football or other games. So, when the other boys went off to play soccer or cricket, Miles could only watch them. That made him very unhappy. But there was nothing he could do to change the situation.

Sometimes, though, he joined in the games they played in Ransome Park after school. The sports master wasn't present then to tell him he wasn't allowed to take part. Miles just had to take care that his mother didn't get to know what he was doing.

Miles was already the tallest boy in his class. And that was one of his big problems because his mother kept saying, 'You've outgrown your strength, Miles'. He was so tall and thin that some of his school mates had a nickname for him: they called him 'Miles High'. They seemed to think it was a terrific joke. Miles didn't mind too much; some boys had worse nicknames than that. Jackie Barber was known as 'Skinhead' and Ray Gallop was always called 'Horsey'.

As he wasn't able to play very often Miles naturally wasn't much good at football. He knew that – and so did his school mates. All the same, he knew a great deal about soccer. He watched games at all levels as often as possible. On Saturday afternoons he attended matches at the local Second Division ground and he never failed to support the School team when they were playing at home. On Sunday mornings he went to see the Junior League games in

Ransome Park and he never missed any match on television if he could help it. Usually he had to go to bed fairly early because his mother repeatedly pointed out that a growing boy needed plenty of sleep. Fortunately he managed to conceal from her that he often read football magazines under the bedclothes with the help of a pocket torch.

The match which Miles was reporting at that moment and in which Geoff Leyland scored the winning goal had been played that morning. It was one of the Sunday League matches in the park. Geoff played for Wakeley Wanderers, a team Miles wrote about regularly in his newspaper. Several of the players attended his school and they all bought copies of the paper. The team was having a good run and winning most of their matches.

A year ago the team had been so bad they had hardly won a corner kick. Spectators used to yell at them: 'Wake up, Wakeley! You're supposed to go to sleep at night, not during a football match.' All that had changed. Nowadays their supporters roared them on with cries of, 'Whack 'em, Wakeley! You can beat this lot by ten goals.' And sometimes Wakeley actually did score ten goals in a match.

Wanderers had begun to improve from the time Geoff Leyland and another goal-scorer,

Johnnie Evett, had joined the team. At present Wakeley were near the top of their League and had set their hearts on becoming champions.

Miles nibbled at his pencil. He had to make sure the match report was correct in every detail. The Wakeley players would soon tell him if he made a mistake.

Then he began to write: 'Geoff Leyland scored the winning goal for Wanderers in their match against Belville United. It was a brilliant effort. Leyland got the ball just outside the penalty area. He beat one man and then passed to Johnnie Evett. The ball came back to Leyland and he smashed it into the net. It was one of his best goals of the season and it deserved to win any match.'

Miles added some more details about the rest of the game, mentioning as many players by name as possible. Each one referred to in the story was a likely customer when it came to selling the next edition of the paper. With a bit of luck, he might sell as many as sixty copies this time.

After reading through the report Miles thought about the headline. He liked writing headlines, though they weren't always easy to think up – and he could only fit so many words into the available space at the top of the story. After some consideration he pencilled in:

'Wanderers win again'. Then he remembered he'd used that one on another occasion.

He thought again – and had a bright idea. He wrote: 'Leyland hits the winner'. Geoff would be delighted with that, and this time he might buy as many as five copies.

Miles gathered up all his reports and stories and then meticulously checked through every one of them for the last time. If they contained any factual errors they would have to be rooted out now; there wouldn't be another opportunity to spot them before the paper was printed.

When he was satisfied that all was well he gathered the stories together and put them in his school case. When he came down from his bedroom there was no one about to ask him where he was going. In any case, his family knew very well that on Sunday afternoons he always went to see Mrs Jenks, who lived in the next street.

During the week Mrs Jenks worked as a secretary with a big engineering company. Miles liked to imagine that on Sundays she worked as his secretary. For it was she who printed the copies of *Soccer Special* for him. She typed the two pages of the newspaper at home and then took them to her office on Monday. There she used a photo-copying machine and ran off as many copies as Miles wanted. He collected them from her on Monday evening and sold them the next day.

Miles liked Mrs Jenks very much. She was interested in football – which his mother certainly wasn't – and she often called him 'my favourite reporter and budding journalist'. She said she was sure that one day he would become the editor of a big daily newspaper.

Miles had met her one day in the supermarket. She'd knocked down a pile of cans and he helped her to pick them up. After that, he'd offered to carry her shopping for her whenever she needed him. She said she'd be glad of his help. They'd become quite friendly and regularly she supplied him with items of local news for the paper.

It had been a great surprise to him when she'd mentioned that she was a widow. Miles had always supposed that widows were old ladies, and Mrs Jenks was anything but old – and she was very pretty. He hadn't liked, though, to ask what had happened to her husband.

Most weeks he did her shopping for her because, by the time she returned home from work in the evening, the shops were closed; and he also helped her in the garden, though he didn't much enjoy that. Still, it was what Mrs Jenks called a very fair arrangement. 'You help me with the shopping and the garden,' she had said, 'and I help you with your newspaper.' So, instead of paying Miles for his help, Mrs Jenks paid for the photo-copies of *Soccer Special*. He knew that without such an arrangement it would be almost impossible for him to produce the kind of newspaper that people would buy.

When he rang the bell at her home that afternoon he was still trying to work out how many copies he should ask her to print. He wondered whether he dare ask her to do sixty. She had told him that photo-copies were expensive to produce, so he didn't want to waste any. In any case, he liked telling people that he had sold out of the latest edition. He couldn't do that if he had any copies left over at the end of the week.

Mrs Jenks seemed in a very good mood. She gave him some ginger beer and while he drank it she read every story in the paper. He enjoyed watching her reaction. A nod indicated approval, a smile that she had particularly liked a story. Best of all was when she laughed out loud because she'd found a joke or an amusing description of something or somebody. Just occasionally she frowned. That meant she wasn't entirely happy about a phrase he'd used or that he'd failed to express himself clearly. Then they'd discuss ways of improving that story. Not once, though, had she ever suggested that an item should be excluded from the paper because it might offend the person concerned. In fact, she'd once remarked that he had very good taste. Miles wasn't absolutely sure what that meant.

'Very good, Miles,' she smiled. 'It's really full of news this week. You'll sell every copy in no time at all. Will fifty copies be enough, do you think?'

'Well, I was wondering if you could do sixty this week, Mrs Jenks,' he said. 'Sales seem to be going up at the moment, you see.'

To his relief, she agreed without any hesitation.

As he was leaving she gave him a shopping list and some money. He would get the things for her on his way home from school the following evening. Then, just as she was closing the door, he remembered something.

'Oh, Mrs Jenks,' he said hurriedly. 'Could you please add a line after the Wakeley match report? They've got a special challenge match on Friday evening at Ransome Park. It starts at five o'clock. I think we should say, "All spectators welcome". Then, you see, they might get some more supporters. It's a vital match for Wakeley.'

She laughed. 'Okay, Mr Editor. Anything you say!'

Two

The challenge match was against Westhill Albion. Earlier in the season Wakeley had beaten them in a League match by a single goal – a goal scored from the penalty spot. The Westhill players claimed they'd been robbed; it should never have been a penalty in the first place, they insisted. Wanderers, however, had collected the two points and that win had helped them climb up the League table.

In spite of the fact that they, too, were now doing well in the League, Albion hadn't forgotten that controversial defeat. Every time players from the two teams met at school or anywhere else they still argued about the result. Geoff Leyland, now Wanderers' captain, always replied, 'We can beat your lot any time, anywhere. Next time we play you we'll score six.'

'Okay,' replied the Albion captain one day. 'Prove it! We'll play you again in a friendly match. Only it won't be very friendly. We'll squash you into the ground and trample all over you!'

So the challenge match was arranged for a Friday evening in the park. An older boy had been persuaded to referee the game and both teams were absolutely determined this time to win so convincingly that their superiority could never be doubted.

Miles Hansen was just as keen to be at the match – and to write about it in *Soccer Special*. He'd bought a new notebook and wanted to start filling it. He knew some of the Albion players and he hoped that when the next edition of his newspaper was printed they might buy copies. His reputation for writing an honest report was well known by now.

When he arrived at the park a couple of minutes before five o'clock he was glad to see that the match hadn't started. In fact, the teams were still huddled together in two groups on either side of the halfway line. So far there was no sign of any spectators, which was disappointing in view of the publicity he'd given to the match in the paper.

Miles opened his notebook and was just about to start jotting down some details of weather, ground conditions and background to the match when he heard his name being called. He looked up, surprised. Geoff Leyland was coming towards him, holding out a goal-keeper's green jersey.

'Look, Miles,' he said, 'we need a goalie. Colin Ayrton has got measles, the stupid idiot. We didn't know until after school. We haven't had time to find anybody else, so you'll have to play for us. Okay?'

'Me!' Miles swallowed hard. He couldn't believe that Geoff meant it. 'But I can't play in goal! I've never played in goal in my life.'

'That doesn't matter,' replied Geoff, dismissing the objection with a shrug of his shoulders. 'Any fool can play in goal – there's nothing to it. Anyway, all the action will be down at the other end. We're going to hit Albion for six, and I'll probably score all of 'em. So you won't have anything to do in goal for us.'

Miles wished he could believe him. But he remembered the previous match between the two sides when, for several minutes, Albion had attacked continuously and forced a succession of corner kicks.

'Isn't there anyone else, Geoff?' he asked anxiously. 'I mean, couldn't one of the regular supporters help out? Or what about the substitute? Surely he—'

'We didn't bother picking a substitute.

Didn't think we'd need one for this match. And the supporters haven't arrived yet, lazy devils!'

'But—'

'No more buts!' Geoff said curtly. He was beginning to get impatient. 'Look, if you don't play we're down to ten men, and that's no good. You'll be better in goal than anywhere else. Franny Weir will take the dead-ball kicks for you, if there are any. Here's the jersey, and you can borrow my tracksuit trousers if you want. We haven't got a spare pair of shorts.'

Without waiting for any reply he draped the jersey over Miles' head and ran back to the middle to talk to his team about tactics. Numbly, Miles slipped his notebook back into his pocket. He didn't know what he ought to do. He could imagine all too vividly what his mother would say if she could see him with a football jersey in his hands. Yet this really was a marvellous opportunity to play in a real match for a team like Wanderers.

What began to worry him most, however, was the thought of going in goal. If he made a mess of things his team-mates would never forgive him. And, of course, a goalkeeper could never conceal his mistakes. If he let in a soft goal . . .

On the other hand, he told himself, if he

refused to play at all then Geoff and the other boys wouldn't buy any more copies of *Soccer Special*. That would be a complete disaster.

Really, he had no choice in the matter.

Slowly he made his way towards the net. There he took off his jacket and tie and pulled the green jersey over his head. Franny Weir, the right full-back, dashed up and handed him a pair of tracksuit trousers. Miles changed into them while Franny, grinningly, provided him with some cover – though he was aware that no one was watching him.

Somehow, changing into real football gear made him feel a lot better. He jumped up and down on the goal-line and tried to touch the crossbar. His one worry now was his footwear. Naturally, no one had a spare pair of boots to lend him and so he would have to play in his shoes. Fortunately, the ground was quite dry and therefore the absence of studs shouldn't make too great a difference. Inevitably, though, his shoes would suffer when he had to kick the ball.

Geoff, now standing in the centre-circle with the ball at his feet, turned and waved encouragingly to him. Miles waved back. He just hoped that Geoff would keep his promise and score a bagful of goals. It wouldn't matter so much, then, if Miles let in one or two . . .

The referee blew his whistle to start the match – and Miles immediately began to feel terribly nervous. His heart was thumping and his stomach churning madly. From all the football books he'd read he knew very well that even top players confessed to having butterflies in their stomachs before a vital match, so such a reaction was really quite normal. None the less, Miles found himself wishing that he, too, had measles like Colin Ayrton and could go straight home.

Luckily, it was Wanderers who launched the first attack. Geoff Leyland was intent on keeping his promise before half-time! He and Johnnie Evett, an extremely clever ball-player, combined brilliantly to cut deep into the Albion defence. In the first minute of the game they won a corner.

Albion were unable to clear the ball and it bobbed about dangerously in their penalty area. Miles began to sympathize with the plight of his fellow goalkeeper as it seemed that Wanderers must score. Yet, somehow, Albion kept them out. Wanderers piled on more and more pressure and even their full-backs moved up to join in the stream of attacks.

That simply increased Miles' worries. Now there was no one in front of him, no one to give him any cover. He yelled to Franny to drop back but if Franny heard the call he ignored it.

Then, after five minutes, Wakeley at last managed to get the ball into the net. And, of course, it was Geoff Leyland who put it there – from a pass by Evett. Together they returned to the centre circle in jubilant fashion with Geoff still punching his fist into the air to signal his success. Miles felt relief rather than anything else: at least things were going in Wakeley's favour so far. Albion would have to score twice to win.

When Albion kicked off they showed they weren't going to waste any time in scoring the equaliser. The ball was hammered upfield and three of their forwards raced towards the penalty area.

It seemed to Miles that his co-defenders were slow to fall back. But there was no time to point that out to them. He himself had to make an instant decision: whether to move out to challenge the man in possession or to stay on his line. Desperately he tried to remember what top goalkeepers did in such a situation.

He hesitated – and suddenly the ball was swept out to the left-wing. Franny Weir tried a sliding tackle, and missed completely as the winger jinked round him. Without even looking up the Albion player belted the ball into the middle. It bounced just inside the box.

'Come out, goalie!' Geoff yelled frantically as his centre-half failed to get the ball away.

Miles dashed forth, his arms spread wide. But he hadn't moved quickly enough. Albion's centre-forward reached the ball first and, very skilfully, hooked it over Miles' head.

It was the sort of shot that a boy of his limited experience would probably miss nine times out of ten. But this was the tenth time. For the ball dropped just under the crossbar and rolled into the net.

So, before Miles had even touched the ball in

the match, Albion had scored. Wakeley's one goal advantage had been wiped out almost immediately. The teams were level again.

Geoff himself marched up the pitch to pick the ball out of the net. He looked thoroughly disgusted.

'Stop dreaming,' he said cuttingly to Miles. 'Concentrate on what you're supposed to be doing. It's no good me scoring at the other end if you're going to let 'em in at this end. Waste of time, that is.'

'Sorry, Geoff,' Miles muttered. He felt terrible and just as upset as Geoff. He was as keen as any of the other Wanderers to win this challenge match. There was no point in trying to make excuses for his failure to prevent Albion's goal. He had, as Geoff had told him, to concentrate on his particular job throughout the game.

That goal had a wonderful effect on the Albion players. Any sense of inferiority they had when playing Wanderers had vanished. They felt they were as good as their opponents, and their goal had proved it. Their confidence soared, especially as they believed that Wanderers' goalkeeper was useless. So they should be able to score again. That thought made all the difference to their attitude to the rest of the match.

When one of their half-backs won a tussle for the ball in the centre-circle Albion were on the attack once more. Inspired by his goal, their chief striker dribbled towards the penalty area before passing to a colleague.

Wakeley tried to marshal their defence but couldn't prevent one attacker from breaking through.

The Albion player was a strong runner with an equally strong shot. As soon as he had clear sight of the net he hit the ball for all he was worth.

Miles had little enough time to see the ball but he flung himself at it. Luck was on his side this time. The ball struck his arm and bounced over the top for a corner kick. As Miles picked himself up Johnnie Evett ran in to pat him on the shoulder.

'Great save, Miles, great save,' he said. 'Keep it up, goalie!'

Miles knew he'd been lucky but that save gave him confidence. He had at least kept the ball out of the net. Then, when the corner kick came over, he used his height to jump and catch the ball. Bouncing it a couple of times in a professional manner, he then carried it for three steps before carefully kicking upfield.

It was amazing. That save had made him feel like a real goalkeeper!

It had also amazed the Albion forwards. In their next attack they attempted to get closer to the goal-line before trying a shot. Again, Miles didn't hesitate. Hurling himself at the inside-right's feet, he grabbed the ball and pulled it into his chest. In the process he took a knock on the shoulder but he hardly felt it as he cleared his line with a kick. This time the praise came from Geoff Leyland himself.

From then on Miles was without fear when the Albion forwards came storming towards him. His height was a great advantage when the ball was in the air; and when it was on the ground he was prepared to dive full-length.

As their attacks broke down and they failed to score a second goal Albion seemed to lose some of their fire. When the half-time whistle sounded it was Wanderers who were clearly on top again and pressing for the lead.

During a spell of inactivity Miles had been thinking that he should use some of the interval to make notes for his newspaper report on the match. He would have no difficulty in describing Geoff's goal but he knew it wasn't going to be easy to write about Albion's equaliser without saying something about Wakeley's goalkeeper. That was going to be the really tricky bit.

As it turned out, however, there was no time to jot down even one word. For Geoff wanted to talk to him on the subject of goalkeeping. As a leading goal-scorer, Wakeley's captain thought he knew a lot about goalkeepers, so he passed on a few tips.

'Just keep your eye on the ball all the time. Don't look at the players or anything else,' was one bit of advice. 'Don't worry about getting hurt, either. You'll soon get over it if you do get a knock. Nobody gets killed in a soccer match.'

Had Miles been thinking clearly, that reference to injuries might have worried him a lot. But he was simply accepting everything that Geoff told him. After all, Geoff Leyland was the captain, the chief goal-scorer and the side's tactician. He was also the fittest boy Miles had ever seen, with tremendously powerful calf and thigh muscles. He looked every centimetre the complete footballer.

When the second half began Miles soon found himself in action again. Albion were awarded a free kick just outside the box. Wanderers formed the usual defensive wall. Miles couldn't see anything of the ball or the player who was about to take the kick. So he yelled frantically to his own defenders to let him see what was happening. He'd remembered that all League goalkeepers did that when a free kick was being taken from close range.

Rather grudgingly, the defenders responded by shuffling fractionally to one side.

The Albion half-back who took the kick produced an astonishingly powerful shot. Had it been straight it might have gone into the roof of the net. But the ball just flicked against one of the defenders. That took some of the pace off it – and the ball swerved away to the right. Miles hadn't lost sight of it for an instant.

He threw himself across the goal and with his fingertips just managed to push the ball round the post. It was the sort of save a Wembley crowd would have greeted with a roar of cheering. His colleagues did their best to match that sort of applause.

After that superb effort, Miles had a fairly easy time for the remainder of the match. Wanderers, combining well in mid-field, set up a series of attacks whereas Albion seemed dispirited following their failure to beat Miles again. Then, two minutes from the end,

Johnnie Evett scored the winner in a goal-mouth scramble.

Wakeley had beaten off Albion's challenge.

As they left the field Geoff put his arm round Miles' shoulders.

'Great goalkeeping, kid, great goalkeeping,' he said with evident sincerity. 'That save from the free kick was out of this world. As far as I'm concerned Colin Ayrton can have measles and chickenpox and swamp fever and anything else he likes for the rest of the season. You'll take over from him in goal on Sunday when we play Sellerby Rangers.'

Three

The following morning Miles was sitting at his desk in his bedroom trying to write a report on the challenge match. It was what to say about the goalkeeper, himself, that was troubling him. For a newcomer the goalie had played – there was no other word for it – brilliantly (apart from that first mistake, of course). But Miles didn't think it would be right to describe his performance in that way. The rest of the Wakeley players would think he was simply being big-headed. On the other hand, though, he had to keep up his reputation for honest and impartial reporting.

Then, of course, there was the matter of naming Wanderers' goalkeeper. If he used his own name his parents would soon know that he had been playing football. Usually, his mother skipped some of the details of the soccer reports but his father read every line. Vividly, he could imagine his parents' combined reaction.

Miles considered the idea of making up a name. That would certainly solve the problem as far as he himself was concerned in spite of the fact that he would like to be seen to have shared the glory of Wakeley's great victory. Yet, he feared that his team-mates would treat such a stratagem with suspicion. They might think it was just another way of showing-off.

He was still wrestling with the problem when, without even knocking, his sister burst into the room. She was flourishing a copy of the latest issue of *Soccer Special* and plainly she was very angry.

'Miles, you've been spying on me! And I don't like it. I don't want my private life written up in your silly newspaper every week for everyone to read about and joke about!'

'I haven't been spying on you, Rosemary,' Miles protested. He didn't even know what she was talking about.

She thrust the paper in front of his face and pointed with one finger at a story in the Personal Column. It read: 'Rosemary Hansen seems to have a new boyfriend. They were seen talking together for a long time by the Park gates. They were holding hands. Martin, her old boyfriend, hasn't been to visit her for some days. More news about this later.'

'Look, it's nothing to do with you who I meet,' she went on bitingly. 'It just causes trouble when you write things like that.'

'Oh, why?' Miles asked innocently.

'You know very well why! I know you sell copies to Martin when he comes here. So you can just keep quiet about me, understand?'

'It's my job to report the news, *all* the news,' Miles pointed out.

'Sometimes there are things that people don't want put in the paper – things about themselves. Probably one day you'll want to keep something out of the paper about yourself. Some things are *private*, Miles.'

Miles didn't make any reply to that. He knew how true it was. So he simply nodded.

'Good,' said Rosemary, smiling for the first time since she'd entered the Editor's office. 'I'm glad you understand, Miles. So just remember to keep me out of your paper in future.'

She seemed to be on the point of departing when she added, 'By the way, how's your typewriter fund coming along?'

She was referring to the money he was trying to save to buy his own typewriter. And he knew very well why she had mentioned it at this moment.

'Sorry, Rosemary, but that's no good,' he

said bluntly. 'You can't *pay* me to keep news out of the paper. That would be dishonest!'

She spun round and went out of the room without another word, slamming the door behind her. Miles winced at the noise. But he wasn't worried by her remarks. In any case, he was sure she would continue to buy copies of the paper. She'd be even keener in future to see if he had written anything about her.

One minor point did trouble him, however. If Martin had ceased to be her boyfriend Miles would have lost a customer. Miles quite liked him, though they were never able to discuss soccer together for Martin was a rugby player.

Suddenly, Miles remembered that when rugby teams included a new player, and they didn't want other teams to know his identity, they often gave him a special name: A.N. Other. And that, Miles decided, was the perfect answer to his own problem. Wakeley Wanderers' new goalkeeper could be described as A.N. Other.

He had written the first two paragraphs of his report. Now he started on the third: 'Wanderers brought in a new goalkeeper, A.N. Other. He made a bad mistake and let Albion score their only goal, the equalizer. But after that he played quite well and made some good stops. Colin Ayrton couldn't play because he has measles. His team-mates hope he'll soon be better.'

After that, the rest of the report was easy to write. Miles, too, hoped that Colin would soon be well again; but he also secretly hoped that Colin wouldn't be fit enough to play again just yet.

For Miles was greatly looking forward to keeping his place in goal for Wanderers. It had been a marvellous experience to turn out for a *real* football team in a Cup-tie atmosphere. It was very much better than just watching a match and writing about it.

At first, he had been scared of two things: first that he might get hurt, for everyone recognized that goalkeeping was a dangerous job. Whenever a goalie dived at a forward's feet there was a risk that the attacker might kick him instead of the ball. Miles had taken such a knock but had hardly felt it. Perhaps, therefore, he was tougher than anybody imagined.

Secondly, he'd been scared that he might let the team down by making stupid mistakes. He had made one big error, when Albion scored, but in the second half he knew he'd done quite well. When he'd made that save from the free kick he'd felt great: it was as good as scoring a goal. For preventing goals was as important as scoring them.

His big worry now about the game on Sunday was not whether he would play well. It was whether he could keep it a secret from his parents that he was taking part in a League match and not simply reporting it.

All he could hope was that none of his family would stroll through Ransome Park the following morning and pause to watch the game between Sellerby Rangers and Wakeley Wanderers.

Four

Sunday was living up to its name; the sun was shining so brilliantly it might have been midsummer's day. Miles, as he hurried through the Park, was thinking that the pitch was sure to be hard. Goalkeepers preferred softer conditions. There was less risk of getting hurt when it was muddy.

For this match he didn't have to worry about his shoes, however. He had borrowed a pair of boots from a friend who took the same size as himself in footwear. The friend was one of his customers and Miles had promised to let him have the next three issues of *Soccer Special* free of charge in return for the loan of the boots.

Most of the Wakeley players had their own kit and so Geoff Leyland was going to lend Miles a spare pair of shorts. He had also kept the goalkeeper's green jersey for him.

'Hi, Miles High,' Geoff grinned when he saw him. It was a joke he liked to crack as often as possible. 'Are you in good form today? We don't want to let in any goals against this lot, you know.'

'I feel great,' Miles told him. And he did. He was also feeling just a little nervous but he wasn't going to admit that. He wanted Geoff to think that the Wanderers' goalkeeper was capable of stopping anything.

Geoff began to tell him about the Sellerby forwards and Miles listened carefully to every word. It was very useful to know what sort of players he would be facing. For instance, Rowlandson, their centre-forward, was well-built and almost as tall as Miles. He used his weight a lot and was very dangerous in the penalty area.

Rowlandson liked to think he was a good header of the ball but, Geoff continued, *he* didn't think much of Rowlandson's ability in that direction. In his opinion, Sellerby's best player was the inside-left, a small ginger-haired boy called Reed. Unusually for a schoolboy, Ginger Reed could hit the ball well with either foot. In spite of his size, he possessed a hard shot.

'You have to know about these things when you're the captain,' Geoff added. 'You've got to think about this game of football – use your brains all the time. If you know a player can use only one foot then you know how to tackle him.'

Miles nodded. He was very impressed with Geoff's knowledge and he appreciated being given such information. But more than that he was grateful for the sense of confidence Geoff had given him. Already he had been made to feel part of the team, part of Wakeley Wanderers. It was obvious now that Leyland regarded him as a capable goalkeeper. So Miles was determined not to let him down. The best way of doing that was by not letting in any goals.

As usual, the players went into the bushes to change before going out on to the pitch. Miles couldn't help thinking that it would be marvellous one day to put on his football kit in a real dressing-room at the ground of a Football League club. Pegs to hang clothes on, bench seats round the walls, oranges and cool drinks at half-time, hot showers after the match – fantastic!

When the referee arrived he called the captains together to toss for choice of ends. It was Geoff who called correctly and he decided to play with the sun behind him.

Sellerby, wearing an all-blue strip and clearly eager to make a good start, forced a corner with their first attack. Ginger Reed, showing good ball control, cut in from the left, beating two defenders on the way. To keep him out of the box Franny Weir turned the ball over the line.

Miles didn't feel at all nervous. He was glad of the chance of being in action right from the start. He knew that top goalkeepers liked to 'get a feel of the ball as soon as possible' (as television commentators were always saying). But the kick was not a good one: the ball didn't even reach the edge of the penalty area.

Yet Miles couldn't relax his concentration. For Ginger Reed had dropped back intelligently and when the ball came towards him he deliberately punted it high into the air. It was going to land close to the penalty spot.

Miles judged that it was a goalkeeper's ball. So he didn't hesitate. Moving swiftly off his line, he jumped high to catch the ball. He hadn't taken his eye off it, and so he didn't notice that Rowlandson was also determined to reach the ball.

They collided in mid-air. Miles had just managed to grab hold of the ball in the split-second before they touched and as he fell the big centre-forward came down on top of him. Miles was winded and almost let the ball roll from his grasp. Rowlandson was quickly on his feet and tried to kick the ball out of Miles'

hands. He'd sensed a chance of a goal and he wasn't going to miss it.

The referee blew furiously. Rowlandson, startled, stepped back as the official dashed up to him. He tried to give the impression that he couldn't possibly imagine what was wrong. But the referee left him in no doubt with a severe reprimand for dangerous play.

'You might have caused a serious injury,' he told the subdued Rowlandson. 'If you attempt anything like that again you'll be sent off in double-quick time. Understand?'

Rowlandson nodded and trudged away from the box. Miles was still struggling to his feet. Luckily, he wasn't really injured, although he felt shaken. After all, Rowlandson wasn't exactly a bag of feathers.

Franny Weir took the free kick so that Miles could have more time to recover. For the next few minutes it was Wakeley who set up the attacks and they ought to have scored. Twice Johnnie Evett went close to giving his side the lead but each time he was foiled just when it seemed certain he would get the ball in the net. After the second near-miss Geoff Leyland was seen to be indicating that he himself would have done better in such a situation.

With all the activity concentrated at the other end of the pitch Miles, already feeling perfectly fit again, had time to look round. One or two people walking through the Park had paused to watch the match. But Miles didn't recognize any of them. He was rather hoping that he might spot some of his *Soccer Special* customers. They would surely be impressed to see that the Editor was not only attending the match in his journalistic capacity; he was also playing in it.

He was just turning away to resume his concentration on the game when he saw someone he did know, walking along one of the paths that bordered the pitch. His heart almost stopped.

It was Rosemary!

She was strolling, hand in hand, with her new boyfriend, the one Miles wasn't supposed to mention in his paper. To his dismay, they were heading in his direction.

If she noticed him it could only lead to trouble. There could hardly be any doubt about that. Even if she didn't mention to their mother that she'd seen him playing football she could hold that threat over him for as long as she liked. Moreover, she might let slip the news at home without intending to whenever the subject of football cropped up. And that, he knew, would be the end of his playing career.

Rosemary and her companion were now

close to his end of the pitch. They appeared to be completely absorbed by one another but Miles couldn't afford to take any risks at all. He turned and, as casually as possible, wandered across to the other side of the penalty area. He wanted to put as much distance as possible between himself and his sister. As he heard her laugh at something her new friend had said Miles winced.

If only he could make sure they didn't see his face . . .

He didn't suppose they would recognize him instantly in a goalkeeper's jersey but nothing had to be left to chance. So he lifted his right arm across his face as though he were about to wipe some sweat away. But he kept it there.

Accordingly, Miles wasn't aware of what was happening at that moment in the game. He couldn't see that Rangers had at last broken out of defence, and that some of their forwards were dashing forward in support of a colleague who had the ball. Most of the Wakeley defenders were in the wrong half of the pitch, having gone up to join their forwards. So, when the ball was slipped to Ginger Reed, the Sellerby inside-forward had almost a clear route to goal.

Easily Ginger took the ball round the one defender who was on hand to try and challenge him. Glancing up, he saw that Wakeley's goal-keeper was well off his line and not even watching the play.

From just outside the penalty area Reed took careful aim and hit his shot with as much force as he could muster. The ball bounced before it entered the net but it was a goal all the way. With so much space to shoot at Ginger could hardly have missed.

The ball was just crossing the line when, at last, Miles looked up. He had heard the frantic calls of 'Goalie! Goalie!' from Geoff Leyland. But he didn't immediately realize what they meant.

In any case, his first thought was to find out whether Rosemary had seen him. He needn't have worried. By now Rosemary and her new friend were some distance away and it was obvious that they were still far too interested in each other to notice a game of football.

Miles was horrified to discover that Rangers had scored. As, sad and shaken, he went to retrieve the ball from the net Geoff Leyland rushed up to him. The expression on his face suggested that he would willingly commit murder.

'What on earth were you doing?' he yelled from a distance of less than a metre. 'That was the softest goal anybody ever scored! You just gave it to them, Hansen, just presented it to them on a plate. You must be mad, standing there with your hands over your eyes. What were you thinking about, man?'

'Nothing, Geoff, nothing at all,' Miles mumbled. There was nothing else he could say. Geoff had every right to tear into him. Had their positions been reversed Miles would have done the same.

Leyland had to get back to the centre-circle to kick off again. As he set off he issued a chilling warning.

'Don't do anything so stupid again. *Concentrate* on the game and don't take your eye off the ball *for a second*. Or else . . .'

Miles nodded and edged backwards to his goal-line. In a few moments the disaster began to take second place to a feeling of relief. His secret, he was sure, was safe. No one would be mentioning to his mother that he was playing football in the Sunday League. Rosemary and the mystery man were now out of sight. Miles didn't think there was much likelihood of their returning by the same route.

Wanderers were determined to get the equalizer without delay. Sweeping into the attack, they sent their left-winger off on a strong run down his own flank. As an opponent tried to dispossess him he cut inside and passed to Johnnie Evett. The inside-forward sent a defender the wrong way with a clever dummy and then slipped the ball to Geoff Leyland.

Geoff hit it on the half-volley and deserved a goal for his effort but he was foiled by a fine, diving save by the Rangers goalkeeper. Wanderers' captain flung his arms in the air in despair. Miles could imagine just what his team-mate was thinking at that moment about goal-keepers in general and two of them in particular.

In spite of their furious raids and inventive approach play Wakeley couldn't get the ball into the net. Twice they hit the woodwork and on another occasion a full-back kicked off the line with the goalie beaten.

So, when half-time was signalled, Wanderers were still a goal down – the goal that had been scored because of Miles' mistake. The two teams split up into separate groups to discuss tactics for the second half.

Miles went up to join his team-mates but nobody spoke to him. They seemed to be deliberately ignoring him. Geoff, of course, was talking away, explaining what had to be done to save the match. He felt that at least three goals would be needed.

Then, glancing at Miles, he added, 'Of course, we might need more, if our goalie lets us down again by giving away stupid goals. So we must attack right from the kick-off.'

Miles turned away. He felt dreadful again.

Sellerby Rangers were also determined to attack as soon as the second-half began. They knew that one goal might not be enough to win the match and they thought that Wakeley's goalkeeper could be beaten easily.

The centre-forward, Rowlandson, tore into the defence like a bulldozer. He couldn't control the ball for long but when he lost it Ginger Reed was in attendance to seize on it. He took it forward only a couple of paces before lobbing it high into the goalmouth. He'd sensed the sort of trouble that tactic might cause.

For when Miles looked up to follow the flight of the ball he was at once dazzled by the sun. He couldn't see a thing and he had to close his eyes against the glare. That was just what Ginger had expected to happen. Now, with the sun almost directly behind him, Rowlandson was able to jump for the ball. He headed it well.

Miles, now trying to glimpse something of what was going on in front of him, was still having trouble with the sun but he threw his arms up as some sort of cover. The ball struck his outstretched right hand and then spun high over the crossbar for a corner. It was an exceedingly lucky save, as Miles would later admit, but the ball had been kept out of the net. That was all that mattered.

As Reed dashed away to take the corner kick Miles was startled to hear someone behind him calling his name. He turned to discover that it was Mrs Jenks. Before he could say anything to her she took off the green-and-yellow cap she was wearing and handed it to him. It was a very smart cap with a big peak.

'Put it on, Miles,' she said. 'It'll keep the sun out of your eyes.'

He did so, tugging it well down over his forehead. To his surprise, it fitted him quite well. There was time only to grin his thanks at Mrs Jenks before he turned away to deal with the corner kick.

Ginger put all his strength into the kick and succeeded in floating the ball into the penalty area. A defender managed to get his head to it and tried to clear the danger. He, too, was troubled by the sun and he could only head the ball upwards.

Miles didn't hesitate any longer. 'Mine!' he yelled as he raced forth and, jumping high, he caught the ball cleanly. Then he bounced it a couple of times, dodged round an attacker and cleared upfield. It was a most efficient piece of work. The sun hadn't bothered him at all.

'Well done, Miles,' said Mrs Jenks, still standing behind his net. 'I think you've been keeping secrets from me. Obviously, you've played in goal before today. I must say, I was a bit surprised when I noticed who was wearing that rather nice green jersey. I'd expected to see you standing near the halfway line with notebook and pencil in hand.'

There was no time for Miles to make a reply. Sellerby Rangers were attacking again. Ginger Reed was having a marvellous match and was the inspiration of the latest venture deep into the Wakeley half of the pitch. Keeping the ball right at his toes, he dribbled past two defenders and reached the edge of the penalty area. Momentarily, he slowed up as Franny Weir went in to tackle him; then he darted away again to his right.

Franny was determined not to be beaten again by Rangers' crafty inside-forward. Chasing after him, he lunged at the ball. But he missed it completely and knocked Ginger to the ground.

The little red-haired player wasn't hurt and immediately he leapt to his feet, protesting loudly that he'd been fouled inside the box.

'Penalty, ref! Penalty,' he yelled.

To Ginger's delight, the referee agreed with him. Blowing his whistle, he pointed in dramatic fashion to the spot. Franny Weir started to object in frenzied fashion but it was Geoff Leyland who silenced him. Geoff knew that there was nothing to be gained by arguing with a referee who'd made a firm decision.

For the second time that afternoon Miles was horror-struck. He thought for a moment that his heart had stopped. Then it started to bang away, louder than ever. He swallowed hard. Often he'd wondered, as he watched a match on television, how a goalkeeper felt when he

was about to face a penalty kick. Now he was finding out.

Ginger Reed was taking the kick himself. Miles crouched on his line, trying to guess which way Reed would shoot. Ginger hit the ball with his right foot, though not as hard as he'd planned. The ball kept fairly low and was going to the left of the goalie.

Miles was able to watch it all the way but he had to dive to reach it. His height enabled him to get his hands to the ball and he managed to push it out. He was getting to his knees as the ball, having bounced against the upright, rolled back towards him. Gratefully, Miles scooped it up as Ginger rushed towards him.

He could hardly believe that he'd made such an excellent save but the yells of delight from his team-mates confirmed his success.

'Great save, Miles, great save!' Geoff sang

out to him. Miles jogged forward a couple of paces and then confidently booted the ball up-field.

'My goodness, that was really something!' Mrs Jenks exclaimed. Miles had almost forgotten that she was there. 'After that, I can see I'm watching a future England goalkeeper!'

He grinned at that. Yet, he admitted to himself, it would make a nice story for his paper – if he dare be so immodest as to use it. No, on second thoughts, he couldn't possibly quote that remark.

His penalty save seemed to have put fresh heart into Wanderers as well as shaken their opponents. For, within two minutes, Wakeley had netted the equalizer.

Once again, it was Johnnie Evett who was responsible for much of the build-up to the goal. He was given good support by the left-winger but when the ball was forced into the penalty area Geoff Leyland it was who crashed the ball into the net.

Rangers were badly rattled. Until Miles' penalty save they had felt to be on top. Now nothing would go right for them. Miles himself was just a spectator as the Wakeley forwards pounded away at the opposite end of the pitch. Another goal just had to come and it arrived with only five minutes left to play.

Geoff was making one of his characteristic storming runs through the middle when a Rangers full-back charged into him just inside the box. Wakeley's captain crashed to the ground and the referee, up with play as usual, had no hesitation in awarding the second penalty kick of the afternoon. Normally, Geoff would have taken the kick himself but he had hurt his knee in the fall. He tried to hobble about for a moment or two and then had to sit down.

Miles knew that Geoff really must be in pain and unable to kick the ball. Not for any other reason would he have surrendered his chance of scoring another goal.

So Johnnie Evett was entrusted with the responsibility of taking the kick. Miles closed his eyes and crossed his fingers. If Wanderers scored they would surely win the match and collect two vital points to help them up the League table.

Johnnie took a very long run and then slid the ball very calmly into the bottom right-hand corner of the net. The goalie had been given no chance at all of matching Miles' save.

That was the final score: 2–1 to Wakeley Wanderers. Miles joined in the whoops of delight as the referee signalled the end of the game. He raced across the pitch to join his team-mates and everyone congratulated everyone else.

In spite of the fact that his knee was still worrying him Geoff Leyland was in high spirits.

'Well done, Miles High,' he grinned. 'That save of yours kept us in the match. It was crucial. If Rangers had scored then we'd have been in dead trouble. Dead trouble. So keep up the good work in the next match.'

Somebody pointed to the cap Miles was wearing. 'I think that brought us a bit of luck,' he remarked. 'You'd better wear it next week as well.'

Until that moment Miles had completely forgotten he was wearing it. Guiltily, he thought he should return it right away. Fortunately, Mrs Jenks was still in sight, strolling along the path beside the pitch on her way home. He ran across to hand it over to her.

'Well, I'm glad I was able to help,' she said as she put it back on her own head. 'But in future, young Miles, you'd better have a cap of your own to keep the sun out of your eyes. Tell you what, I'll buy you one for Christmas – a real goalkeeper's hat. I think you deserve one. Then everyone—'

Miles gulped as he struggled to speak. 'Thanks a lot, Mrs Jenks. But I don't think I'll be playing again. You see, my mother says—'

'Oh, I know what you've always told me about your mother,' said Mrs Jenks, cutting him off. 'But I expect she was thinking about you dashing all over the place in the middle of the field and getting over-tired. It's different when you play in goal. You don't use up so much energy, for one thing. Instead you use skill and judgement.'

Miles didn't know what to say. But Mrs Jenks hadn't finished yet.

'Anyway,' she added, 'I think you're a lot fitter than she imagines. And I'm going to tell her so.'

Miles hardly knew what to say but his hopes suddenly began to rise.

'Do you mean that, Mrs Jenks? You'll ask her if I can continue playing for Wakeley?'

'Of course I will, Miles. I'll also tell her how much hard work you do for me in the garden and carrying those heavy shopping bags. That *proves* you're very fit. She might as well know, too, what a very fine goalkeeper you are and that your team needs you.

'So, nip off and get changed quickly and I'll walk home with you. Your mother's in for a bit of a surprise, I reckon.'

Five

Horrified was the word Mrs Hansen used to describe her reaction to the news. Judging by the expression on her face, Miles was well aware that she meant it, too. He knew that there was no hope of her rescinding her decision to ban him from playing football.

'It's your treachery that horrifies me as much as anything, Miles,' she said as soon as Mrs Jenks had left. 'You've been so very, very underhand in what you've done.'

'But, Mum, it was the only way I could *prove* I was fit,' Miles pointed out. 'The one sure way to prove you're fit to play football is actually to play in a game, a real, hard, competitive game with boys who're playing all the time. And I didn't come to any harm – you can see that for yourself, Mum. I mean, look at me. I look perfectly healthy, don't I? And I feel great, just great. Physically, I mean.'

'I've told you before, Miles, appearances

aren't everything,' she replied with no hint of any sympathy for his point of view in her voice. 'A person can feel perfectly well one minute and quite wretched the next. It's happened with you before. A boy of your age is no judge of what's best for him in health matters, especially when you're so tall for your age. As Dr Moray said, you've simply outgrown—'

'—my strength,' Miles muttered wearily. He really was sick to death of hearing that phrase. 'But, Mum, he said that *ages* ago! I haven't been ill for years. So Dr Moray doesn't know how fit I've become. I'm sure he wouldn't say that if he'd seen me playing for Wanderers today.'

Suddenly, he remembered something he'd heard his parents discussing over lunch. 'Hey, it's tomorrow night, isn't it, that Dr Moray's coming round to play cards with you and Dad? Well, then, you could ask him to give me a check-up before you start. I mean, I'm sure he wouldn't mind if *you* asked him, even if it is his night off.'

'Oh no, Miles,' his mother said firmly, shaking her head with great solemnity. 'I wouldn't dream of imposing on Dr Moray in that way. When he comes here for an evening of cards it's a relaxation for him – and a doctor needs complete relaxation like everyone else. Dr Moray is

59

a friend of the family, a very good friend, and one doesn't make use of friends for that sort of purpose except in an extreme emergency.'

'He may be your friend, and Dad's, but he's no friend of mine,' Miles murmured truculently. 'Last time he was here he wouldn't even buy a copy of *Soccer Special*. Said he ought to get a free one for services rendered, whatever that means.'

'That's quite enough, Miles!' his mother said sharply. 'I won't have you insulting Dr Moray after all he's done for you. He's a very fine medical man and I trust him implicitly. Now, you can get off upstairs and have a proper lie down. Rest is more important than ever after what you've been up to. Go on now, off you go.'

He was halfway up the stairs when she called out with fresh instructions. 'On second thoughts, you'd better have a hot bath immediately. After all the running about you've been doing there's bound to be the risk of a chill. So you must have a bath. And, Miles, that means you're not to go out of the house again today.'

At the top of the stairs Miles uttered the worst curses he could think of as loudly as he dared. Then, after slamming home the bolt on the bathroom door, he turned both taps full on.

As the water gushed into the bath he slowly stripped off his clothes and tried to think constructively about the latest disaster in his life.

He realized now that it would have been better if he hadn't accepted Mrs Jenks' offer to speak on his behalf to his mother. It was obvious that his mother resented what she said was Mrs Jenks' interference in the matter of his health, something she claimed to understand better than any outsider possibly could. Miles didn't believe that was true but he was hardly in a position to dispute it; when his mother made a pronouncement like that there was simply no arguing with her.

No, what he should have done was just to mention casually at home, when he was sure no one was really listening properly, that he'd given Wanderers a bit of a hand when they had a problem to sort out. That was the truth. It was unlikely that anyone would have asked for further details or suspected that Miles' hands had been sticking out of the sleeves of a goalkeeper's jersey. Then, if the subject had ever cropped up again, he could have protested, with absolute sincerity, that he'd told them he was helping the team. It might have been weeks before any member of his family learned that he was playing football regularly and, by then, he would have had real proof that it was doing him no harm at all.

He hated being accused of treachery and he supposed that was why he had retaliated with his remark about Dr Moray. That, he recognized, had probably done him a lot of harm. On the other hand, he wasn't sorry he'd criticized the man. He didn't like him and he had a feeling it was mutual.

As he stretched full-length in the bath and allowed his chin to sink to the level of the water, Miles switched his thoughts to the team, *his* team as he'd begun to think of Wakeley Wanderers. By not playing for them again he would be letting them down. Geoff Leyland and the other players had never really understood why he wasn't allowed to play soccer; so now, when he told them he'd played his last game for them, they'd be even more puzzled. Geoff himself was a fitness fanatic, always had been, and it was his opinion that everyone could be as fit as he was (well, *nearly* as fit) if they took the trouble, as he did, to go through a regular routine of strength-building exercises. He'd tried to impress that on his teammates but only a couple of them followed his example.

Of course, with luck Wanderers should have their regular goalkeeper back for the next match. By then Colin Ayrton should have recovered from his bout of measles and be ready to return to the team. Whether he'd really be match-fit was another matter. Miles allowed himself a rueful grin as he reflected on that situation; for in his own mind he had no doubt at all that he himself was completely match-fit. On top of that Geoff made it plain that he regarded Miles as the better goalkeeper; so if both players were available for the next match Miles would be the one selected to play. In those circumstances, poor Colin might just as well have remained on the sick list!

Miles tugged the plug fiercely from the bath, stepped out and slowly began to dry himself. There was one consoling thought: he still had *Soccer Special*. No one was going to take that away from him. Writing about football wasn't the same as playing football but it was the next best thing. His newspaper gave him the freedom to say whatever he wanted about any person and any team.

It occurred to him as he went into his bedroom that in the next issue he could write about his own performance in the Sellerby match. Now that his parents knew what he'd been up to there was no longer any need to conceal his identity. He could discard 'A.N.

Other' and give the credit for that penalty save to the player who'd made it: Miles Hansen. His team-mates would think it strange if he didn't. They expected the editor to highlight brilliant saves as well as brilliant goals. He wouldn't, however, mention that it was Hansen's last appearance in Wanderers' colours. That would only look as though he was pleading for sympathy. His brief career as a goal-keeper was over; but his editorship would continue. From now on it was his job to build up circulation and make *Soccer Special* required reading for everyone he knew. Success as an editor would help make up for all the disappointments he'd suffered in his efforts to become a footballer.

After making some notes for the Sellerby match report he put down his pencil and started to think about the sort of features his readers might like to find in the paper. Naturally, the subject of soccer came first. But what could he write about that was original and newsworthy and that everyone would want to read? It was no good picking one of the teams he normally wrote about or even one of their star players. That would arouse only limited interest. No, it had to be a team everyone knew even if they didn't support it . . .

Got it! Athletic, the town's Second Division

club, now in a mid-table position. Miles grinned with delight at the idea of writing about a professional team: it was an inspiration. So far as he could tell, the boys at his school were completely divided on the subject of Athletic. Half of them believed that the team had a real chance of promotion that season, the other half were convinced they were certainties for relegation.

So it was obvious that both halves would be interested to know what actually went on at Highdale, Athletic's famous ground on the outskirts of the town. If he could arrange to interview Dave Rosborough, the team's Manager, and get his personal views on the club's prospects for the season it would be a marvellous story. Best of all, it would be an 'exclusive' story, and that was something he'd always wanted to write in *Soccer Special*. An exclusive about Athletic ought to guarantee that the next edition of the paper would be a sell-out even after printing extra copies.

Miles had never been behind the scenes, as he thought of it, at a professional football club, though often enough he'd wondered what real dressing-rooms would be like, and the Manager's office, and the treatment room, and the huge bath into which, so he'd heard, all the players dived after a match. Now, if Athletic agreed to allow him to visit their ground, he could describe everything he saw in great detail. With luck, he might even get a chance to talk to some of the players. Maybe one of them would even be willing to write a special article for the paper – and autograph it so that every reader would recognize that it was yet another *Soccer Special* exclusive.

There wasn't a moment to be wasted. Miles turned to a fresh page on his notepad and began to draft the vital letter.

Dear Mr Rosborough,

I would very much like to interview you for my newspaper, *Soccer Special*. It would be an 'exclusive' article and I know it would interest all my readers. Many of them attend the same school as I do and they all take a great interest in Athletic. So they would be fascinated by any news I could give them of the team and of yourself.

I know that you are very busy every day but if you could spare me about half-an-hour of your time one day very soon I would be very grateful. School finishes at 3.30 p.m. and I could be at Highdale within twenty minutes.

I do hope you will agree to be interviewed by me. I look forward to meeting you very much.

All best wishes to Athletic.

Yours sincerely,
Miles Hansen

Word by word he went over what he'd written and decided he really couldn't improve on it. His English teacher, had he seen the letter, would have disapproved, no doubt, of the excessive use of the word 'very' but Miles himself wasn't worried about that; he preferred to let his enthusiasm show through. According to Press reports that Miles had read, 'enthusiasm' was one of the chief attributes Dave Rosborough expected to find in his players and staff so he would certainly look for it in a newspaper reporter who wanted to interview him.

Miles hurried along to his sister's bedroom to persuade her to let him have a sheet of writing-paper, envelope and stamp. Rosemary, who was doing something to her hair, handed them over without any inquiry at all about why he wanted them (he'd been sure she'd ask who on earth he was writing to). She seemed to be in a blissful mood and Miles correctly concluded it was entirely due to the effect her new boyfriend was having on her.

After writing the letter, and signing it with a flourish, he propped it against his school case to be posted the following morning. If all went well it would be delivered on Tuesday and thus there was a distinct chance he might receive a reply on Wednesday. He crossed his fingers on both hands.

Dave Rosborough didn't let him down. His letter arrived second post on Wednesday and was handed to Miles by his mother when he returned home from school. Although she didn't say anything she appeared to be expecting him to tell her what it contained. He tried to look nonchalant as he opened it but his heart was thudding with excited anticipation.

Dear Miles,

Thanks for your letter. Yes, I'll be pleased to give you an interview for your newspaper. Let's make it Friday of this week. I'll expect you about four o'clock.

If you'd like to bring a pal with you (your Assistant Editor perhaps) that'll be okay. But only one, please – not the whole class!

Also, perhaps you'd bring a copy of *Soccer Special*. I'd very much like to see it.

Looking forward to meeting you on Friday,

> Yours in sport,
> Dave Rosborough
> Manager

When Miles glanced at his mother he saw that her eyebrows were raised.

'Oh, it's nothing much,' he explained, folding the letter and putting it back in its envelope. 'Just something about my newspaper.'

It was only when he reached the privacy of his own bedroom that he let his feelings explode in a whoop of joy.

Six

Geoff Leyland really did look as delighted as he said he felt. He and Miles had dashed headlong to the bus stop as soon as school was over on Friday afternoon and now they were trying to get their breath back as, impatiently, they waited for the Highdale bus to arrive. Several times already he had said what a great, fantastic, brilliant, super-splendid idea it was to fix up an interview with Athletic's Manager. Miles glowed with satisfaction as well as with his exertions on the way to the bus stop. He would always be grateful to Geoff for allowing him to play those couple of matches for Wakeley Wanderers; now, by taking Geoff with him to Highdale, he was repaying some of that debt of gratitude.

Almost literally, Geoff had jumped at the chance of meeting Dave Rosborough when Miles had shown him the letter. Although he himself was hardly one of Athletic's most faithful supporters, Geoff was quick to point out that he'd always admired their Manager because, 'when he was a player with Arsenal and Northampton he was one of the fittest men that ever kicked a ball – that's what my Dad says, anyway.' Miles hadn't questioned that judgement. It was a well known fact that Geoff's father, a county squash player, was the ultimate authority on the subject of physical fitness. Geoff made sure that every acquaintance of his was aware of it.

'Anything he tells us when he shows us round the place will be useful and probably we can include some of their ideas in our own training routines,' Geoff had added confidently as he accepted Miles' invitation. 'So I'll make a note of what he says about getting really fit for a big match. I'll remember to take my own notebook with me.'

'Well, that'll certainly make you look just like an assistant editor. Dave Rosborough will be impressed when we both take notes,' grinned Miles.

'Hey, don't tell him that's what I'm supposed to be!' Geoff protested. 'I mean, English isn't exactly my best subject, you know. I like to do things, not just write about 'em.'

Then, realizing what he'd said, he hastily added, 'Oh, sorry, Miles. I wasn't getting at you personally. Anyway, you do both, don't you – write about the team as well as play for it.'

Miles had made no reply to that. So far he hadn't been able to bring himself to the point of mentioning the ban on playing for Wakeley Wanderers or any other team. He was well aware that there wasn't one chance in a hundred that he'd be granted a reprieve but he sensed that by telling Geoff what had happened he'd be admitting total defeat. In any case, Mrs Jenks had advised him not to give up hope, 'Because *something* – I don't know what, but something – could turn up and cause your mother to change her mind at the last minute. We ladies have a habit of changing our minds, you know!' Mrs Jenks was full of sympathy for his plight and said that she was responsible for it. So, in compensation, as she put it, she'd produced an extra twenty copies of the paper that week and Miles had managed to sell every one of them.

However, he'd kept two copies to give to Athletic's Manager and, as he and Geoff hurried to the ground after dropping off the bus, he checked that they were still safe in his pocket.

When they reached the 'Players' and Officials' Entrance' Geoff stood aside for Miles to enter first – and Miles couldn't help grinning to himself at that because it was probably the first time in his life that Geoff Leyland had deferred to a team-mate.

To the right of the entrance hall was a high glass-topped counter and behind it was an elderly man apparently totting up some figures in a thick black ledger. After giving them a quick glance he continued with his counting until he'd reached the bottom of the page. Then, with a look of irritation, he slid back a glass shutter and brusquely asked them what they wanted.

'We've come to see the Manager, Mr Rosborough,' Miles explained. 'He's expecting us.'

'Oh, is he?' said the man in obvious disbelief. 'I doubt that. If it's one of those schoolboy trials you're after then you've come on the wrong day at the wrong time. They're on Wednesdays. And you've got to write in and ask for one. You can't just turn up here without warning and expect us to fit you in at your convenience. So you're wasting your time turning up here like this. Best be off and apply through the proper channels.'

Miles was thoroughly dismayed. 'But, you see—'

The glass shutter was being thrust back into

the closed position when a door opened at the far end of the room behind the old man and Dave Rosborough came into view.

'Thank goodness for that!' Geoff muttered. 'Another half-minute and we'd've been thrown out of the place.'

The Manager caught sight of them, smiled broadly and indicated that they should go through the swing doors to their left. This time it was Geoff Leyland who led the way.

They were in a corridor that stretched as far as they could see in both directions. A moment later Dave Rosborough emerged from the reception area and shook hands warmly with each of them.

'Don't let old Jack put you off,' he said breezily, jerking his thumb towards the room he'd just left. 'He's getting on a bit and when we're short-staffed he's not exactly the sweetest-tempered chap you've ever met. But he's been a loyal supporter of Athletic for over fifty years and that's what counts.'

Still chatting affably about the club and its staff, he led the way along the corridor to a door which bore the word 'Manager' in white lettering on a transparent plastic plate. Ushering them into the office, he told them to make themselves at home and ask any questions they liked.

'I meet the Press boys regularly and sometimes they give me a hard time after we've had a bad result,' Mr Rosborough added. 'So I've had to learn to cope with tough grillings from sports writers like yourselves!'

Miles decided that this was the right moment to hand over the copies of *Soccer Special* and they were received with evident interest. While the Manager scanned them Miles glanced round

the office. It was much smaller than he'd imagined and contained only a plain desk, three chairs, a metal filing cabinet, a small cupboard and, the only surprise, a pile of yellow-and-green football shirts that obviously were brand new. Yet Athletic's normal colours were red-and-white. Miles had also expected that their host would be attired in a red tracksuit for he'd often been described in the local paper as 'a typical tracksuit manager, one who always takes part in training sessions with his players.' On this Friday afternoon, however, the former Arsenal and Northampton winger was casually dressed in a polo neck sweater and a sports jacket in broad checks.

'Well, this is a very professional effort,' said the Manager, laying the copies of the newspaper on his desk. 'I'm really very impressed. What made you start it up, Miles?'

'Well, I had a lot of illnesses when I was younger and I used to get bored with nothing to do when I was getting better. I liked writing about real things – in English lessons at school, you know – so that's why I began to make up a newspaper. I like thinking up headlines as well.'

'You look pretty fit to me now, Miles,' Mr Rosborough remarked.

'He plays football for my team now,' put in Geoff Leyland. He felt he was in danger of being left out of the conversation altogether. 'That's Wakeley Wanderers and we're in the Sunday League. Miles is the goalie.'

'Good,' said the Manager approvingly. 'You've certainly got the right build for a goalkeeper. To my mind, he has one of the most important jobs in the team.'

He paused, and then went on, 'Look, boys, how would you like it if I showed you round now? You can ask your questions while we're on the move; some of the things you see just might give you some fresh ideas. Anyway, I think better when I'm on my feet instead of being stuck behind a desk. So maybe you'll get some smarter answers that way!'

Eagerly they followed him into the corridor which, he explained, ran the full length of the main grandstand. 'Right above our heads are the posh seats, the most expensive ones, and the directors' box – oh, and next to that is the Press box. I must remember to show that to you, Miles. You might have a seat there yourself one day.'

Further along the marathon corridor they came to the players' dressing-room – but Miles' attention had been caught by a football, suspended by a long cord from the ceiling, just above an adult's head height. Spotting the boy's interest Dave Rosborough jumped from a standing position and neatly headed the ball forward and upwards.

'Just a fun thing really,' the Manager

grinned. 'But it helps to keep the players on their toes. Few of them can resist practising a header when they're walking down this corridor. Plenty of visitors like to have a bash at it, too.'

The home team's dressing-room wasn't as interesting as they'd hoped it would be. It was unoccupied and there wasn't so much as a single shirt hanging up on any of the pegs round the walls and the benches were just as bare of boots and football gear. What it did possess, though, was a faint odour of ointment and antiseptics, a smell which Miles remembered vividly from times when he'd received medical treatment. He was glad to move into a connecting room – only to be confronted by what he recognized as an operating table!

'Don't look so aghast, we don't cut anybody up on that!' Mr Rosborough said cheerfully, correctly interpreting Miles' thoughts. 'It's just an ordinary treatment table such as you'll find in every football club today. This gleaming equipment over here is for providing special heat rays. They're marvellous for clearing up bruises and deep-seated strains in muscles. We have a physiotherapist who comes in when we need him and he's the expert on all the stuff we've got in here for dealing with sprains and knocks.'

He opened a tall white-painted cupboard and the boys stared in awe at the contents: bandages, tubular sleeving ('a special kind of bandage to give extra protection to ankles – a very vulnerable spot for footballers, as you'll know'), jars of oils and Vaseline, sticking plasters, tapes, cans of antibiotic sprays and pain-killing sprays, and even boxes of chewing gum.

'Here, catch!' Dave Rosborough called, tossing each of them a packet of chewing gum. Automatically, they both pocketed them, not to be eaten later but kept as souvenirs of their visit to Highdale.

'You wouldn't think we'd need all that medical stuff when you see what we do to get the players fit in the first place,' the Manager remarked as they accompanied him further along the corridor and into a large gymnasium. With its wall-bars and pile of mats to land on it greatly reminded Miles of the one at his school but some of the equipment he'd never seen before anywhere.

'That's the thing that really pinpoints any player's strengths and weaknesses,' said Rosborough, nodding towards a device that appeared to consist of gleaming metal bars and levers, pulleys and iron weights and leather support straps and harness. In height it was taller than the Manager and to Geoff it resembled a rather crazy geometrical design. He voiced that thought.

'Maybe so,' Dave Rosborough laughed, 'but it does a great job in testing a man's physical resources and co-ordination. Or a boy's, for that matter. Want to have a go and see for yourself?'

'Sure thing,' said Geoff, stepping forward eagerly and slipping off his jacket. The Manager showed him how to lie at the foot of the machine, his feet slightly higher than his head on a narrow board that would pivot when the correct pressure was applied. After checking that Geoff's ankles were comfortably positioned in leather slings the Manager made some adjustments to the balanced weights and then told him to start pressing down.

Within seconds the strain of Geoff's efforts to lift the weights began to show on his face. Soon he was sweating quite freely and he looked to be in anguish.

'I don't think – I've quite got the – the hang of this,' he gasped. And Miles laughed. He knew the pun hadn't been intended but he couldn't help being amused by it. Geoff tried to glare at him but succeeded only in making his grimaces look even more grotesque.

'Don't overdo it,' Dave Rosborough said warningly. 'Better relax now, Geoff.'

Wakeley Wanderers' captain relaxed so quickly that the weights clanged against each other noisily. After being released from the slings it was a moment or two before he staggered to his feet.

'It's my knee, you see, Dave,' he mumbled. 'I hurt it in the last match and perhaps it's not quite right yet. In fact, I'm still getting a bit of pain in it.'

'Yes, well, it's just been confirmed that you aren't one hundred per cent yet in your leg muscles,' the Manager told him. 'This machine is designed to find out exactly those sort of weaknesses. For any player, the one certain cure is rest – and you shouldn't need much of that at your age.'

He turned to Miles. 'Do you want to have a go, Mr Editor?'

Miles was no less enthusiastic than Geoff had been and promptly settled himself into position to be tested in the identical exercise. After pausing for a few moments to relax himself completely, he began to exert the necessary pressure with his thighs and legs. To his delight, the weights moved appreciably and he had by no means exhausted himself.

'Well done, Miles!' Dave Rosborough called. 'Didn't take you long to learn proper co-ordination. But that's far enough, I think.'

Geoff was scowling at him as Miles stood up and when the Manager asked if they'd like to have a go at anything else it was Geoff who responded first. The next exercise was aimed at developing strength and suppleness of shoulder and arm muscles. 'Because a footballer,' they were told, 'has to be healthy in every part of his body, not just in his legs and feet. In soccer all the body comes into play during a true, competitive game.'

Again it was Geoff who went into the harness first, determined to prove his superiority over Miles. But the performances, which this time were actually recorded on a dial by electronic digits, were practically identical. If anything, Miles, much to his surprise and delight, had the slightly better score.

'Well, that really proves how fit you are, Miles,' Dave Rosborough said admiringly. 'And it's just as well because a goalie has got to be tough, really tough. But I can see you'll make the grade all right if you keep up the good work.'

Miles grinned his appreciation of the compliments but he daren't look at Geoff. He could sense his friend's reaction to such praise after he himself had been told he lacked complete fitness. To Geoff, that really was a case of adding insult to injury.

After a quick glance at the players' lounge ('this is where they can relax both before and after a game') and the boardroom, where the directors of the club met to discuss business matters and the team's performances, the boys were taken up into the main stand and shown the Press box. Miles was fascinated to learn that some of the reporters had their own private telephones so that they could ring through reports to their offices during the game or immediately it was over. The phones were kept on a shelf under the sloping wooden ledge, rather like an old fashioned school desk, that served as a writing table.

'So this is where you may sit one day, Miles, when your own playing career is over and you're working as the sports editor of a big national paper,' the Manager smiled. 'I just hope that you'll be reporting that we went to the top of the League after thrashing Manchester United, or Liverpool, or Spurs by six goals to nil!'

Miles thought he detected a hint in all that and so, at last, he started to ask the questions he'd prepared the previous evening. Dave Rosborough, perching on the edge of the box, took care to give a precise answer to each one – and Miles, having no knowledge of shorthand, was thankful that he didn't speak too quickly.

He'd been worrying that he wouldn't be able to get down half of what he was told.

Once or twice it seemed to Miles that Geoff was on the point of interrupting with a question of his own so each time he shot him a warning glance. He guessed that the Manager, who'd so far been very generous with his time, had other things to do that afternoon and Miles didn't want to outstay his welcome.

Eventually, however, Geoff had to say something. He felt he'd been left out of the conversation long enough.

'I thought we might be meeting one or two of the first-teamers, Dave. I mean, I wouldn't have minded a chat with a couple of the strikers. We could've discussed ways of getting through tight defences.'

The Manager smiled sympathetically. 'Not on a Friday afternoon, young man. All the first team squad go home early on a Friday in readiness for tomorrow's match. Gives me a chance to catch up with paperwork and so on. You wouldn't believe how many forms and things I have to sign in a week.

'No, the only players who come in at this time are those who need special treatment for injuries and so on. Luckily, everyone's fit at the moment. Which is a happy, if rare, state of affairs. Injuries, especially those that don't quickly respond to treatment, are really what play havoc with a manager's plans.'

'Yeah, I know. I mean, it's the same with us—'

'Look, I think we'd better be off,' said Miles hurriedly, cutting off Geoff's meanders. 'We're very grateful to you, Mr Rosborough, for giving us so much of your time. It's been great seeing round a club like Athletic. And I know my readers will be fascinated to hear about your views on the team's prospects.'

'Delighted to have you,' replied the Manager, keeping in step with his visitors but leading them towards the exit. 'And don't forget, Miles, I shall be looking forward to seeing the article in your newspaper.'

'Oh, I won't forget, Mr Rosborough. I'll send you two copies as soon as they're printed. You should get them on Tuesday – or Wednesday at the latest.'

The Manager accompanied them to the players' entrance, shook hands with them and wished their team luck in its next match.

Geoff had little to say until they reached the bus stop. It was unusual for him to be so subdued but Miles didn't comment on it. He was already thinking about the article he was going to write. He would enjoy underlining the exclusiveness of it by reporting that: 'The Manager himself told me . . .'

'You know something?' Geoff said suddenly. 'I don't believe Dave Rosborough knows what he's talking about.'

'Eh?' Miles was thoroughly startled.

'Not about injuries, anyway,' Geoff continued as though Miles hadn't uttered a sound. 'It's crazy to say that you're fitter than I am – crazy! I've always been the fittest player in the team by miles – and that's not a joke, Hansen. You aren't in the same street as me when it comes to *real* fitness.'

'But, Geoff, I've just proved it – you saw what happened on that machine . . .'

'Rubbish! That wasn't working properly. Or probably Dave didn't know how to set the balances and things. I'm not having it said that I'm not fit. So I'm going to prove, *really prove*, that you don't stand a chance with me in a *genuine* fitness contest.'

'But how? How?'

Geoff, eyes narrowing, gave him a hard look.

'Now, just listen to this . . .'

Seven

It was even colder – much colder – than Miles had feared it would be. Under his borrowed tracksuit he was wearing a long-sleeved sweater as well as a woollen shirt but somehow the wind was still getting right through to his bones. Or, at least, that was what it felt like. He shivered and told himself he was crazy. When he found that he was nodding in agreement with himself he shook his head angrily. For the umpteenth time he wished he'd been bold enough to resist Geoff Leyland's challenge.

He had actually been on the point of laughing off the whole idea when Geoff had suggested he didn't have the nerve for it. That was the word that had really stuck in Miles' throat.

'Nerve!' he'd protested. 'Of course I've got the nerve to try it. The one thing goalkeepers must have is strong nerves. It's the most – the most *dangerous* job in football.'

'Maybe, but having the nerve for tackling a

real Army assault course in the dark from start to finish is different,' Geoff had continued relentlessly. 'That takes real courage, real guts – not your sort of quick grab in the penalty area. You've got to be dead cool with nerves of steel to do what I'm going to do on Sunday night. If you chicken-out, Miles, it'll prove for ever that you can't match me in fitness or in mental toughness!'

'Right then, Leyland, I'll do it!'

As soon as the words were out of his mouth Miles wished he could have swallowed them. But then he'd seen the expression on Geoff's face: a mixture of triumph and wariness. So, after all, perhaps the great fitness fanatic wasn't absolutely confident of success.

Now, as he tried to keep warm at the bus stop while waiting for his rival to join him, Miles took comfort from one stroke of luck. It was a night of the full moon. So at least they should be able to see where they were going; and that was of vital importance if they were going to come through this venture un-scathed.

He had only a rough idea of what was in-volved in competing over the abandoned assault course at Daleside. Like many boys at his school he had taken a brief interest in the Army camp on the edge of the moors above the town. When a party of them had gone up there one summer afternoon they'd hoped to catch a glimpse of tanks and armoured cars and perhaps even rocket-launchers. But apart from Land-Rovers fitted with signalling equipment and a few heavy trucks they'd seen very little of real interest. There'd been rumours in the town that before long the Army would be moving out altogether and already some parts of the camp had been closed down.

The main section of the assault course had been constructed in a wood that clung to an unexpectedly steep hillside. It was some distance from the camp itself and that, of course, was why it was accessible to the public nowadays. According to Geoff, who had reconnoitred it on several occasions, some parts of it were almost hidden by undergrowth but he insisted that it was still in a fit state to be used. He had listed some of the obstacles: a tunnel made of barbed wire which had to be crawled through at speed (and speed, he pointed out, was what it was all about anyway); a deep pit that had to be crossed by poles made out of saplings; wide, water-filled trenches which you swung yourself across on ropes suspended from tree branches; a maze of sharp stakes, all placed very close to each other; and a high thorn fence similar to those found on steeplechase circuits.

'It's really quite formidable,' Geoff had warned him delightedly.

Miles didn't doubt that. But he doubted his ability to complete the course. All he could hope was that Geoff would have problems, too, in spite of his belief that he could overcome any obstacle.

There was confidence in Geoff's very stride, however, as he marched up to the bus stop and then, slipping the pack from his back, wriggled his shoulders. After swinging it freely a couple of times to demonstrate its quite obvious weight he tugged the harness over his shoulders again before leaning, with studied nonchalance, against the signpost.

'Feeling on top form, then?' he inquired.

'Oh, sure, just great,' Miles told him flatly. 'Just great. Ready for anything, you might say.'

'No trouble in getting away? I mean, we don't want a hue and cry like those times when your Ma suspected you might be playing football after school. Had everybody going round in circles when that happened.'

'No worries,' said Miles, annoyed that those embarrassing days should still be remembered. 'I told 'em I had to go and see a pal to compare notes on that farming project we're doing. Said I'd probably be late because it involves masses of research.'

Geoff nodded his approval and started to whistle rather tunelessly. Miles couldn't bring himself to ask whether Geoff had difficulties in disappearing in the evening when he wanted to. He knew that his rival would instantly produce some utterly plausible story.

His curiosity had been aroused, though, by the size of that pack. He asked what it contained.

'Oh, various useful things for an expedition like this. Torch, groundsheet (got that from my brother who had it when he was in the Army), vacuum flask of drinking chocolate and, er, running shoes. Spiked running shoes.'

'Hey, that's not fair!' Miles protested. 'Spikes'll give you an advantage. I haven't got any.'

'It's perfectly fair,' Geoff assured him coldly. 'You could've used 'em if you'd thought about it. I'm a good planner, that's all. Pay attention to planning and the battle's half won – that's what my brother learned in the Army and it makes fairly good sense.'

Before Miles could argue the point further the bus arrived. Geoff athletically leapt aboard first, paid the fares for both of them and refused to accept any contribution to the cost from Miles.

'It was my idea and so I'm quite willing to pay the expenses,' he explained. 'It wouldn't be right for you to pay to be beaten.' He paused, then added, 'But you can pay on the way back, if you like. The winner ought not to have to cough up for everything!'

The journey should have taken no more than half-an-hour but the driver seemed to be conducting a private go-slow campaign so it was almost forty-five minutes before they reached their destination. Miles, beginning to worry about how late it was going to be before he got home, wanted to push on with all speed as they began to climb the deeply rutted track to the moor. Geoff, however, refused to be hurried. It was essential, he pointed out, to conserve their energy because they were going to need all they possessed for the assault course itself.

'Your knee's not still bothering you, is it?' asked Miles, undecided whether he wanted the answer to be yes or no.

'Of course not!' was the spirited reply, accompanied by a vigorous flexing of the joint. 'I've told you, this mustn't be rushed, Miles. Honestly, I don't think you've any idea what you're committed to.'

Another twenty minutes passed before Miles saw for himself what was in store for them. When they entered the wood it was so dark that progress would have been practically impossible without the aid of Geoff's torchlight. But soon the trees began to thin out and it was just possible to see by the light of the moon.

'Lots of the trees were chopped down to make way for the assault course,' Geoff explained. 'There has to be room, you see, for several men to have a go at the same time. With us it'll just be a case of follow-my-leader. That's *you* following *me*, I mean!'

'That's what you think,' Miles told him with a sudden surge of determination. 'I'll just overtake you when I feel like it.'

Not deigning to answer that, Geoff led the way to the first obstacle on the horseshoe-shaped circuit. It wasn't easy to see just what had to be attempted for, to Miles, it seemed to consist of a shapeless mass of barbed wire, much of it inextricably entangled with ferns and bracken and even exposed roots of trees.

Geoff, poking around with a stick he'd picked up, said it was all perfectly clear even though it was in bad shape. He shone his torch to show what he meant.

'It's a series of tunnels, each one made out of the wire. Look, they're in parallel lines. I think those two side-by-side in the middle are the best. All we've got to do is crawl through from one end to the other as fast as possible. Then—'

'But one of those tunnels as you call them seems to have caved-in in the middle. Whoever goes through that one will get stuck in all that wire. I bet it's as sharp as a razor, too. And it seems very narrow.'

'It's wide enough to take a soldier in full battle-gear – you know, automatic rifle, helmet, back-pack. So it's bound to be big enough for us – and especially you, thin as a walking-stick!'

'Thank you very much, *captain*!' Miles answered with all the sarcasm he could muster. He thought of reminding Leyland that it was only a few days ago that his slimness and height had proved rather useful to Wakeley Wanderers; but he realized there was nothing to be gained by that when Geoff was in such an overbearing mood.

'Right, I'll show you what's in store for us next,' continued Geoff, marching off briskly towards the second obstacle.

It consisted of four saplings, each completely stripped of any branches and foliage, laid across an open (and, as far as Miles could tell, bottomless) pit. He guessed that it wouldn't be easy to cross from one side to the other in daylight, let alone in semi-darkness. One false step and you'd be a gonner . . .

'This one should be right up your street,' Geoff was telling him blithely. 'You weigh so little that the pole won't bend much in the middle when you cross. With a heavier, better-muscled bloke like me it's bound to give a bit in the middle.' He paused and then added, 'I'll have further to go, you see, if it bends – so you'll have an advantage on this obstacle. Still, you're going to need some advantages when you're up against me!'

'Weight won't come into it when you're going at speed,' Miles pointed out mildly. 'I mean, balance will be the important thing. One false step and, well . . .'

'Oh no!' Geoff yelled. Then, very theatrically, he groaned. 'You don't *walk* across it, or *run* across it, you idiot! You swing yourself along with your *hands*, like a monkey on the top bar of its cage. It's a long way down to the bottom and I reckon it'll be pretty muddy down there as well. So it would be fatal to try and cross any other way. The whole idea of this obstacle is to test the strength of your arms, of your grip. Get it?'

'Oh,' murmured Miles. He should have thought of that.

'What comes next?' he inquired, anxious to put that blunder out of his mind.

'Oh, just the wall jump. But it's not worth looking at now. There's nothing to it because it's not even very high. You're supposed to take it in your stride. Come on, we'll go on to the fourth.'

Geoff was still chortling about Miles' mistake when they reached the next obstruction: the fearsomely-sharp mass of stakes that appeared to have been planted in haphazard fashion but which, on closer examination, proved to have been placed with quite fiendish ingenuity. For it was just impossible to pass through them in anything like a straight line. To make any progress at all a competitor had to duck and weave from side to side while finding the easiest, and shortest, route. To add to the difficulties, the stakes were of different heights.

'It'll be a bit like playing touch-rugby and trying to swerve past every opponent on the way to scoring a try,' Geoff said complacently. 'Should be fun. You'll also have an advantage in this one as well, Miles High. Being so thin, you should be able to avoid every single stake. Actually, come to think of it, you're almost *thinner* than some of those stakes!'

'If that's what you think – that I have all these advantages – then I can't understand how you expect to win the race.'

'Well, I just want you to have a fair chance. I mean, it should be a handicap really, with you getting some start. But I'll win all right because I'm stronger and fitter. And that's what it's all about, Mr Editor. You'd wish you'd stuck to writing your little paper instead of taking me on over a real, tough, Army assault course.'

By now, Miles was only half-listening. He had been worrying about the time the preliminary survey was taking. They hadn't even started on the race yet and already it was quite late. At this rate, they were going to be out most of the night.

'Look, I think it's time we got started,' he said decisively. 'Let's forget about checking over the course first. I don't think that's necessary. I mean, you've already told me all about it, and the order the obstacles come in. Now I've seen some of them let's get on with the race. Okay?'

'Well, if you want to,' replied Geoff, sounding very doubtful. 'I just don't want you to think you didn't have a fair chance because you hadn't seen the entire course in advance. But if you really want to get cracking . . .'

'Yes! Right away.'

Still Geoff was hesitating. 'Er, but, how about a drink first? I could open that flask of hot chocolate just to—'

'No! Save it till after it's all over. You're going to need it then, *Captain* Leyland.'

It still rankled with Miles that his friend had referred to *Soccer Special* as 'your little paper'. That wasn't Geoff's description when he himself was featured in it. And, doubtless, if he did win the race he would want the full story to be written up, complete with banner headline. Well, Miles was determined Geoff Leyland wasn't going to win; the great fitness fanatic would finish a bad second.

Resignedly now, Geoff was taking off his shoes to replace them with his spiked footwear. As he watched him, Miles' impatience began to ebb. He had a sudden recollection of his mother's expression when she learned that he had been playing football on Sunday morning. Now he could imagine how she would look, and, worse, what she would say if she could see him at that moment. He dreaded the thought that she might, within a matter of hours, discover what he had been doing on the moors. He would be lucky to get back into the house without arousing his parents.

Desperately, he wanted to get the whole thing over with as quickly as possible. It had struck him that this race was both stupid and pointless. Even if he did win he couldn't publicly boast about his success. If he came second he would be a loser twice over because Geoff Leyland certainly wouldn't be inhibited about relating his triumph to everyone who listened to him – in addition, of course, to having the full story published in the paper.

'Come on, come on!' Miles muttered fiercely, clenching his fists.

Startled, Geoff hurriedly got to his feet and didn't even attempt to try out the effectiveness of his spikes. Together they made their way back to the starting point where Wanderers' skipper placed his torch and discarded shoes beside his rucksack. He couldn't, however, resist carrying out a couple of knees-bend exercises and flexing other muscles, just as he did before kicking off in a soccer match.

'Okay,' he said softly. 'I'll give the signal, counting down to zero – and on zero we go, flat out.'

Miles just nodded that he understood. Momentarily, he shivered. It could have been caused by the increasing coldness of the night or by apprehension. It didn't matter which it was. The time for thinking about anything except the race itself had gone.

'Three – two – one – ZERO!'

Geoff shot away even as he was uttering the last syllable.

Miles didn't grudge his rival his start. He was content that Geoff should lead the way over the first few obstacles; but Miles planned to stay on his heels so that Geoff would be aware all the time that he couldn't relax. Then, when the moment seemed right, Miles would overtake him. A race between two people was always a matter of tactics.

Even after choosing the widest tunnel through the barbed wire Geoff wasn't finding it easy to get through to the other side. Twice he snagged his tracksuit top on spikes and there was the sound of ripping cloth as he wrenched himself away from the second one. Miles could hear him cursing his luck.

Not that it was any easier for Miles. At just about the narrowest point of his tunnel he encountered a tangle of brambles wrapped round the wire itself and, as he struggled to make a passage, he wished he'd thought to wear goalkeeper's gloves. His hands were going to be in a terrible state by the time he completed the course.

Using his elbows and knees to push himself along, he was conscious that he was ahead of his rival. Geoff was alternately grunting and muttering and Miles sensed that he had the edge on him when it came to stamina. But that gave him little satisfaction. If the first obstacle was a true indication of what lay ahead of them then it was going to be a punishing course. Physically, they were going to suffer appallingly.

The friction caused by squirming along on his stomach was making him feel sore already and more than once he had to slow up to ease his discomfort.

'I must have been mad, stark raving mad, to have agreed to this,' he told himself.

Then, with a gasp of relief, he was clear of the savage wire. Staggering to his feet, he turned to glance at Geoff.

'Don't blame you for taking – taking that pack off,' he commented as he tried to get his breath back. 'You'd never – never have made it – wearing that.'

Geoff, kicking himself free of the last coil, gave him a look of sheer malice but made no reply. Then, taking a lung-stretching breath, he sprinted towards the poles that spanned the pit. For a moment Miles thought that his challenger was going to attempt the crossing on foot; but, preferring reason to rashness, he sank to his knees and then, taking a firm grip on the pole with both hands, began to work himself across, centimetre by centimetre.

Miles, following his example, soon began to feel that his arms were going to be pulled from their sockets. He'd thought this obstacle would be easier to overcome than the first. It wasn't. All the weight of his body was straining against his shoulder muscles and every fibre of them was signalling its protest at such treatment.

One thing only kept Miles going: the fear of what would happen to him if he relaxed his grip for even a split-second.

At one stage he tried to rest from his exertions. But as soon as he stopped moving the pain in his shoulders became worse. Yet it was just as great an effort to start moving again. The agony was almost unbearable.

He sensed that he needed to concentrate his mind on something else, however momentarily. He and Geoff were back to back as they edged towards their objective; but, by craning his head over his right shoulder, Miles was just able to catch a glimpse of his rival. He saw that Geoff, in spite of starting first, was about a metre behind him. Now grunting, now gasping, Geoff was struggling to keep up.

Miles' elation at being in the lead was short-lived. Even though he had managed to force his body into movement again he was sure he wasn't going to get to the other side of the pit. His muscles were going to collapse under the strain.

'Think ahead ... think ahead ... think ahead,' he kept telling himself. Into his mind

came a picture of a notice he had once seen on someone's desk, a jokey reminder of the need for good planning. The words 'Think Ahead' were printed in large type . . . except for the last three letters which were very small indeed because there wasn't enough space left on the card for them to be printed the same size as the others!

Somehow that silly notice helped him to keep going. For a few moments his mind had ruled his muscles: for those few precious moments the pain had been suppressed. And now he was within a couple of metres of the end of the pole. The torture and the torment were nearly over.

Seconds later, as he slid his right hand along the pole, his hand came into contact with good, moist, black earth. He had made it! Now he needed the strength to heave himself upwards and then claw his way forward until he was again on solid ground. Where he found that strength he never knew. But, at last, the fearful pit was no longer beneath him but behind him.

Still trembling, he turned to see where Geoff was. Although still making a lot of noise, the Wanderers captain seemed to have found his second wind and was swinging towards him at a surprisingly good speed. As he touched the side of the pit Miles tentatively made a move to help his friend up on to firm ground. Then he realized that assistance was the last thing Geoff would want or allow.

Geoff, too, appeared to be shaking as he got to his feet. He also seemed to be struggling to say something. Miles waited to hear what it was. He just hoped that Geoff was going to suggest that they called the whole thing off, that they should settle for an honourable draw or dead-heat or whatever he wanted to call it. After all, they'd both surely proved already that they possessed strength and fitness in abundance.

'Go on, then, go – on,' Geoff gasped. 'I don't need you to – to wait for me. Get on to the next – it's the wall jump.'

Miles' heart plummeted again. He should have known better. Geoff wasn't a boy who would capitulate while there was still a chance of winning.

As Miles hesitated it was Geoff who led the way towards the next obstacle. It was one which Miles hadn't seen but which had been described by Geoff as, 'Dead easy – you just run up a grassy slope, a bit like a ramp, on to the top of a brick wall, then jump off into a sandy trench. Easy, 'cos it's such a soft landing.'

Staggered by his friend's show of renewed energy, Miles followed him at a slower pace. Geoff reached the top of the slope almost before Miles was at the foot.

The leader paused, yelled, 'Here we go!' – then vanished.

Miles was still struggling up the incline when he heard a terrible cry of pain.

Eight

Miles stood on the parapet, peering down into the dark. Vaguely, he could make out something white but couldn't tell what it was. After that one anguished cry, there was no sound from Geoff.

'Geoff, are you down there? Geoff, what's happened? Geoff?'

'Of course I'm here! God, the pain's awful. I've smashed my leg up.'

Geoff's voice was surprisingly close at hand and, after the silence, it startled Miles. His first thought was to jump down beside Geoff.

'Some stupid idiot's filled the trench up with rubbish,' Geoff was calling. It's all over the place. God, I really think I've broken it. Get down here quick, Miles, but watch out where you're going.'

Hurriedly, Miles retreated down the slope and went round the side of the wall. As far as he could tell the trench was full of tree branches, some of them very solid indeed. Gingerly, he made his way to where Geoff was lying.

'Don't move!' he said warningly as Geoff struggled into a sitting position, still clutching his leg just below the knee. He was biting his lip hard and for a moment didn't answer when Miles asked where the pain was.

The question had hardly been necessary. There was a long, jagged rip in the trouser leg of the track suit and blood was oozing from a gash just under the knee. But, to Miles, it didn't look as though the bone was broken.

'We've got to stop the bleeding, that's the first thing,' said Miles, kneeling beside him and reaching into his pocket for a handkerchief. 'I'll tie—'

'Go and get my pack,' Geoff interrupted him. 'I've got a medical kit in there.'

Miles was astonished, and his reaction was visible.

'I brought it for you. I thought you'd be sure to need it,' muttered Geoff. 'Now, go and get it before I bleed to death!'

Skirting the two obstacles on which they'd expended so much time and energy, Miles dashed back to their starting point and grabbed Geoff's pack and the torch which lay beside it. In his experience Geoff had always told the truth and so he really must have carried the first aid kit for Miles' benefit. Yet, in spite of his careful planning, Geoff had failed to check whether the landing zone under the wall was free of danger. Miles knew that, for once, he himself had been very lucky. If he'd jumped first . . .

'It's still bleeding,' the victim greeted him on his return. 'So do something quick.'

Miles cleaned the wound with cotton-wool and then smeared it liberally with antiseptic cream. Apart from wincing and biting his lip Geoff bore the treatment stoically. In such poor light it was hard to tell how shocked he was by the incident but Miles thought he looked whiter than usual. He was thankful his friend hadn't fainted. He'd known other boys do that when they'd seen the extent of their injuries.

'You'd have no trouble getting a job as a medical orderly,' Geoff murmured as Miles started to apply a dressing.

'Oh no, I'd be a top surgeon at least!' Miles grinned.

He was aware that Geoff had started to shiver again, quite fiercely this time, and he knew it was essential to get him into a warm atmosphere as soon as possible.

'Hey, how about some of that hot chocolate?' he suggested. 'We could both do with a drink.'

As he rummaged in the pack he came across something that felt like a pocket watch. But when he drew it out he saw that it was a compass. Well, at least that was one thing they didn't need.

Gratefully they both sipped at the chocolate and presently Geoff admitted that he was beginning to feel a little warmer. But, he added, the pain was still as bad.

'Do you think you'll be able to walk – with my help, I mean?' Miles inquired.

'I'll have to, won't I?' was Geoff's grim reply. 'There's no phone for miles so we can't ring for help. This would happen just when I was winning the race. I'd've won by a street.'

Miles ignored that. He recognized that his rival now needed some consolation.

'Well, we'd better get started, Geoff. Otherwise if your leg starts to stiffen up you may not be able to use it at all. Come on, I'll help you up.'

'Ouch!' yelled Geoff when he made his first attempt to put weight on his injured leg. But for Miles' supporting arm he'd have slumped to the ground again. 'Oh God, it's worse than I thought. I'll have to lie down again.'

'No you won't,' Miles told him sharply. 'That's no good. We've got to start moving.

You can't stay here much longer. It's getting colder for one thing.'

He didn't mention it but it seemed to him that it was also getting darker by the minute. The moon was disappearing behind a cloud formation – or was that mist coming down? Suddenly, Miles began to feel very alarmed; but it was important not to communicate that to his friend.

With one shoulder supporting Geoff's rucksack and the other Geoff himself, Miles only managed to stagger for the first few steps. Geoff was a complete dead weight but, of course, he could do little to help himself. Eventually, Miles adjusted his stride to cope with the situation.

There was no longer any doubt about it. A mist was descending on the moors and accounting for some of the chill in the air. So they might need that compass after all.

'How's it feel now?' he asked so that he could think of something else.

'Rotten. No better at all. I feel a bit sick as well.'

'Well, don't be sick down me if you can help it – I've got enough to support as it is,' Miles joked.

Luckily, they were going downhill in the direction of the lane that would eventually lead them back to the bus stop. Though, Miles feared, it was hardly likely that buses were still running past that spot.

The journey to the lane was a nightmare. Several times they both stumbled and each time, as his foot touched the ground, Geoff let out a yelp of pain.

'I can't go on, I can't,' he cried. 'It's sheer agony, Miles.'

'We've got to keep going,' was the determined answer. 'We've had it if we don't. This mist's getting thicker.'

They staggered on. Miles, crushed by Geoff's weight and thoughts of what might happen to them, often felt like giving up, too. Never had he felt so exhausted; not even in some of his worst illnesses. Every part of him was aching. But he wouldn't relent. His will-power didn't weaken. Even his mother had more than once told him that he possessed real determination to see things through. He kept thinking, too, of what Dave Rosborough had told him about his physical fitness. That was like a bright light that led him on irresistibly.

At last, after what seemed like hours, they entered the lane. Geoff suddenly sagged against him and muttered, 'Let's have a rest now. I must sit down for a bit.'

Miles thought it could be fatal to stop now

but he, too, needed a breather. He refused, though, to allow Geoff to lie on the ground, which was bound to be damp. Instead, he propped him against the drystone wall.

'Look,' Geoff said a few moments later, 'we just can't go on like this. You must be shattered – and my leg's just about killing me. We've got to get help, fast. It'll take ages for both of us to get down to the road. So you go ahead and get somebody to rescue us. Stop the first car you see. Or, better still, find a phone box. Ring somebody to come and fetch us.'

'I'm not leaving you, Geoff!' Miles was appalled by that idea.

'You must! Get to a phone quick, that's the best thing.'

'You mean the police – ambulance . . .'

'No, not them! My folks'll murder me if I get involved with the police, or get them involved rather. Don't ring my home, either. They mustn't know I've been up here. I've been warned off this place umpteen times. When we get home we can say the accident happened somewhere else. What about your parents? Your Dad'd fetch us, wouldn't he?'

'No, not them either!' That suggestion was even more appalling. 'But I'll have to get somebody who'll come quickly. But – but who?'

For a moment or two there was silence.

Then, exasperatedly, Geoff snapped, 'Look, you're supposed to be a newspaper editor. So you should have a load of ideas.'

'Oh! Oh, yes, *of course*. She'll help, I know she will. Oh God, I just hope she's in when I ring.'

'Who d'you mean?'

'Mrs Jenks! My – er – you know, that secretary girl who types the stories for me.'

'Good. Well, go on, go and get her, Miles.'

Still Miles hesitated. 'Okay, but look, Geoff, don't move from here for heaven's sake. If you got lost in this mist we might never find you. So—'

'I won't move because I can't. So get going. And leave the pack with me. I think there's still some chocolate in that flask.'

Miles began to run down the lane. It didn't occur to him that it was almost a miracle that he had energy enough to walk let alone run after what he'd just endured. He was thinking about Mrs Jenks, praying that she wouldn't let him down. She never had, and that was everything. All the same, everything now depended on her being at home. If she wasn't he would simply have to phone his parents and tell them where he was. There'd be no alternative.

Once, on the way down, he stumbled and banged his knee. That made him think of

Geoff and his plight and so resolve to take more care. It would be utter disaster if both of them were injured and unable to walk.

When, with heart-thumping relief, he reached the main road it seemed to him that the mist had lifted a little. But it was eerily quiet. Not a sound of any kind. He paused, wondering which direction to take for he'd no idea where he might find the nearest phone box. Up here on the moors, call boxes would be well spaced out. That seemed crazy to him. There should be *more* telephones in isolated places because that's where they were vital.

He turned left, the direction from which they'd come on the bus – a million years ago that seemed now. He alternated his pace between a fast walk and jogging, continually glancing over his shoulder in hope of seeing the lights of a vehicle.

Then, distantly, he heard the noise of a car engine somewhere behind him. Miles stepped into the middle of the road. It didn't matter how fast it was going, he had to stop it.

The blur of yellow lights came nearer and grew brighter. Miles held his arms wide and, to his intense relief, the car slowed and pulled sharply into the side of the road. Miles dashed forward as, cranking down the window, the driver called, 'What's up?'

When he learned that Miles was asking for a lift to the nearest phone box the driver, a middle-aged man wearing a tweed cap and a scowl, looked even more dubious. He wanted to know who was to be telephoned and why and what Miles was doing out on his own at this time of night in the middle of nowhere; he kept glancing over his shoulder as if expecting someone else suddenly to appear at one of the car's windows. Despairingly, Miles tried to explain that his friend had injured a leg, was immobilized and that they needed to summon a friend, a lady who would know how to cope with the situation.

'Is this lady a nurse?' asked the driver, beginning to sound helpful.

'Oh no!' Miles said, and immediately wished he'd answered differently.

The driver gave him a long look and then, grudgingly, said that Miles could get into the front seat. 'But behave yourself or you won't get very far,' he added to Miles' amazement.

As it was, they'd travelled only a few hundred metres when the headlights picked out a very modern-looking telephone box. At once, the driver braked hard to a halt.

'There you are then,' he said in a tone of triumph mixed with assumed cordiality. 'Hop out. Goodnight.'

Miles barely had time to close the door before the car was speeding away again. He didn't dwell on the strangeness of the driver's attitude; he was just thankful that he wouldn't have far to walk back to where Geoff was lying when he'd made the call to Mrs Jenks. All he could hope now was that she was at home. What he'd do if she wasn't he dare not think.

'Please answer, oh please answer,' he prayed as he listened to the dialling tone. He was so apprehensive he almost dropped the coin he was waiting to push into the slot. It wasn't the cold that was causing him to shiver.

And then he heard her voice. He rammed in the money.

'Mrs Jenks? This is Miles Hansen. I'm at Daleside with Geoff Leyland and he's had an accident and we need your help right away and . . .'

She was marvellous, not interrupting once until he'd completed his story. As always she was the perfect editor's secretary. Afterwards Miles thought it was wonderful that she hadn't suggested (as surely anyone else would have done) that his and Geoff's parents be contacted immediately. But then she was well aware of what Mrs Hansen's reaction would be. Instead, she said it was lucky that she had a friend visiting her and so they could come straight away in his car. All she asked for were precise details of where the boys were so that no time should be lost in locating them.

'Go back to Geoff and help to keep him as warm as possible, Miles. And yourself, too. Don't worry about anything. We'll be there in a flash.'

It took a little longer than that and Geoff, who had found that his leg wouldn't bend at all, had begun to complain bitterly that Miles had done the wrong thing: he should have rung for an ambulance. By now Geoff had forgotten that he'd vetoed that course of action. Miles had insisted that they should try to get closer to the main road to save time. In reality, he feared that Geoff's condition would be aggravated by his remaining motionless in the cold of the lane. So, for some distance, Miles struggled along, supporting Geoff almost to the extent of carrying him. He didn't think about the effort involved; he knew that, very soon, they would be on their way home by car.

Distantly, they heard it arriving. 'Thanks for what you've done, Miles,' Geoff murmured. 'You've been great. I'll never forget it.'

'This is Brian Alton,' was how Mrs Jenks introduced the man with her and he looked rather amused by something until he saw the exhaustion on Geoff's face. Then, without another moment's delay, he gently hoisted Geoff on to his shoulder and assured him that the worst was over.

After that, it seemed to Miles that everything happened with astonishing speed. Mr Alton, it turned out, was an occasional rally driver and he now drove like one. Miles heard him whisper something to Mrs Jenks about the risk of suffering from exposure and he gathered that they were heading straight for hospital.

'But we didn't want to go *there*,' he tried to

protest. 'They'll find out about what we've been doing and we'll be in real trouble, with everybody. That's why I rang you, because you could handle everything on your own and keep it secret!'

'Miles, that's very sweet and flattering of you,' Mrs Jenks smiled. 'But you know – *you*, especially, must know – that health comes first. We've got to check that Geoff doesn't need any further medical help. You've obviously performed miracles but . . .'

It occurred to Miles that he could have asked the man in the tweed cap to take Geoff to hospital. He supposed that would have been the sensible thing to do. So, if Geoff was worse because of the delay, he, Miles, would be the one to blame. And then . . .

The heater was on in the car and Miles was just too drowsy to think about any more implications of their visit to the Army assault course. He was too weary even to keep his eyes open.

Someone was shaking him gently but persistently by the shoulder. He murmured crossly, 'Stop it. I'm asleep.'

'I know, old son, but if you'll just wake up for a minute or two you can then go back to sleep for as long as you like,' a friendly male voice was telling him.

He opened his eyes and saw a man in a white coat. Miles sat up at once. He knew exactly where he was. He was in hospital again. Then he caught sight of someone else: Mrs Jenks. She was smiling warmly at him.

'Miles,' she said softly, 'you're a hero. Dr Grant here has just said so. He just wants to tell you that himself.'

Miles blinked disbelievingly. But the man in the white coat was nodding genially.

'You've been fantastic, old son, fantastic. And the amazing thing is, it doesn't seem to have taken much out of you. Miles, my boy, you're not only tall for your age, you're strong for your age as well. And that's rare, believe me. So you're very, very lucky.'

'And we've got that in writing, Miles,' Mrs Jenks said with a laugh. 'While you were having a nap Dr Grant examined you pretty thoroughly and when I told him about – well, told him about your mother's views – he said he'd be happy to put his findings on paper. So you've got an A1 fitness certificate to prove it!'

'Can I go home now, then?' Miles asked.

'Just as soon as I've finished my check-up now that you're awake,' replied Dr Grant; and willingly Miles submitted himself to the stethoscope and tappings and gentle pressures. The doctor's radiant approval wasn't dimmed by anything.

'What about Geoff?' Miles asked diffidently. Were they saying nothing about him because . . .

'Ah, well, he's been lucky, too – thanks to you,' said Dr Grant. 'But we're keeping him in here for a day or so, just as a precaution, you understand. After all, he did get knocked about a bit and we want to make sure he really is quite sound. You can pop in and see him tomorrow, if you like. I'll be glad to have a chat with you myself. But now I think it's time you went off home to bed. Mr Alton here is going to be your chauffeur again.'

'It's my privilege,' Brian Alton added.

They were almost at the door when suddenly Miles remembered something.

'You've got that note, haven't you?' he asked Mrs Jenks anxiously.

'Certainly have, Miles!' she replied, and held up a white envelope.

'Great,' he said happily.

Nine

One week later Miles was sitting at his desk in his bedroom checking through the news items and stories that would appear in the next edition of *Soccer Special*. One particular article was worrying him. He wished that he could leave it out but he'd given the writer a firm promise that it would appear, and Miles didn't go back on his promises. A responsible Editor always kept his word.

The story was to be date-lined 'Moorlands Hospital, Monday' and was scheduled to appear under the by-line of Geoff Leyland.

It began: 'Miles Hansen saved my life last night. We were having a race over the old Army assault course at Daleside in the dark. When I fell into some junk after jumping . . .'

Miles shook his head. That wouldn't do at all. The story was melodramatic; worse still, it wasn't factually accurate. So it would have to be corrected *and* toned down. Very firmly, he crossed out the first sentence.

Geoff had remained in hospital for twenty-four hours and, apart from his injured leg, had emerged from their escapade without ill-effects. He had written the article while still in bed and pleaded for it to be published. 'After all,' he'd pointed out, 'it *is* news. There must be a lot of rumours flying about and this article will give the facts about what really happened.' So Miles, determined as ever to present the truth about everything, consented to print it; though, of course, as Editor, he had the right to revise any contribution to the paper.

After making one or two further amendments to the article Miles put it on the pile of material that was ready for the printer. He was looking forward to visiting Mrs Jenks later that afternoon, not least because she'd invited him to stay for tea. Brian Alton would be there too, and, Mrs Jenks had hinted, there was every likelihood that he would become a regular customer of *Soccer Special*.

Miles turned his thoughts to that morning's match and the report he was about to write. It had attracted a larger crowd than usual and, to his joyous amazement, among the spectators had been his parents. For his mother was now quite reconciled to the idea of his playing soccer regularly. It was, of course, that medical report from Dr Grant that had done the trick. Dr Grant, too, was going to become a regular reader of *Soccer Special* because he would receive complimentary copies from the grateful Editor.

The fans had enjoyed a brilliant match with plenty of goals to cheer, though Miles himself hadn't let in even one. He'd enjoyed that success almost as much as the other gift from Geoff, which, in the interests of sheer accuracy, simply had to be mentioned.

Miles took a clean sheet of paper and began

to write the match report: 'Wakeley Wanderers had a brilliant 5–0 victory over Craydon Juniors in their vital Sunday League match. Johnnie Evett scored a hat-trick. In the absence of the injured Geoff Leyland, Wanderers were captained for the first time by Miles Hansen.'